A SHOUT IN THE RUINS

ALSO BY KEVIN POWERS

The Yellow Birds

Letter Composed During a Lull in the Fighting

A SHOUT IN THE RUINS

A Novel

KEVIN POWERS

Little, Brown and Company

New York Boston London

Little, Brown and Company
Hachette Book Group
1290 Avenue of the Americas, New York NY 10104
littlebrown.com

First Edition: May 2018

Little, Brown and Company is a division of Hachette Book Group, Inc. The Little, Brown name and logo are trademarks of Hachette Book Group, Inc.

The publisher is not responsible for websites (or their content) that are not owned by the publisher.

The Hachette Speakers Bureau provides a wide range of authors for speaking events. To find out more, go to www.hachettespeakersbureau.com or call (866) 376-6591.

ISBN 978-0-316-55647-7 (hardcover) / 978-0-316-52314-1 (large print) / 978-0-316-44954-0 (signed edition)
LCCN 2017952216

10 9 8 7 6 5 4 3 2 1

LSC-C

Printed in the United States of America

For Pauline and Louise

One of the most pathetic aspects of human history is that every civilization expresses itself most pretentiously, compounds its partial and universal values most convincingly, and claims immortality for its finite existence at the very moment when the decay which leads to death has already begun.

—*Reinhold Niebuhr,* Beyond Tragedy

I will mourn for what fails here.

—*Roger Reeves, "On Visiting the Site of a Slave Massacre in Opelousas"*

A SHOUT IN THE RUINS

ONE

BY 1870, NOT even four full years after the clerk of Chesterfield County, Virginia, officially recorded Emily Reid Levallois's death, rumors of her survival and true whereabouts abounded. It was said by some that you could see her flitting among the Maroons of Great Dismal on their mesic islands, a white face among the black, as straight and slim a figure as the swamp's ageless cypresses. Or that she was now a washerwoman at a boardinghouse in Baltimore. Still others hypothesized that she had escaped a lynch mob and had wound up passing through the two-bit cow towns along the western coast of Florida, until she spent her remaining days leaving tracks along the white sands where the Manatee River meets the blue-green stillness of the gulf. It is not so hard to imagine. The young Emily becomes older. Our certainty diminishes. Every day the same mismatched rows of least and royal terns look out toward a coming storm as small waves roll in and crash against the shore like the inevitable collapse of a trillion minor hills.

Most of these notions never advanced much further than a passing thought. When said out loud they rarely took the form of proposition, almost always of response. But the rumor that stuck was said with a confidence so unquestioned as to almost certainly be wrong: That she had fled south and west toward the hollows of the Blue Ridge while the fire still burned through the embers of the house at Beauvais Plantation. That you could have found her in the highlands there, up above the meadows in the fog, where the spruce and firs grew through the wreckage of the deadfall of the past.

It's easy enough to understand why she tried to disappear. And if the places she was rumored to have gone were merely substitutes for the idea of flight in the scorched minds of those whom she'd abandoned, no matter. Error begets error. That much is clear.

It may well be that the balance of her life, once the flames had turned that old Adam-style house to ash, was lived only in the stories people told about her. And though there is little need to wonder how she eventually ended up, one might ask if, for her, it was a punishment or pardon. Either way, there's no great tragedy for Emily anymore. If tragedy is what she meant to leave behind, she did so as surely as if it had been written in her will, in the delicate cursive her mother taught her, in an ink of blood and ash.

Her father often told her that she was lucky to have been born at all, considering she was conceived in illness as autumn began in '46. The come-and-go heat signaling the end of another Virginia summer had left his wife feeling used up. By the time her mother was sure she was pregnant,

4

the fever had flushed her face a mottled red and her joints felt like linens twisted up and wrung out to dry. Lying in her sickbed, attended by her girl, Aurelia, Lucy Reid passed three nights cursing her throat, the pain in her bones, and the itch. October rained on their tin roof and it shook the first still-green leaves from the sycamore outside her window. For her husband in the adjoining room, it became hard to separate the conditions that caused his beloved wife's discomfort. And though he would always tell his daughter that he loved her, he often wondered whether those three long evenings had been imprinted in his mind and heart and left him with a permanent deficit in his capacity to show her real, meaningful affection.

When she was born the following summer, Aurelia's hands, the palms of which were rough and pink, were the first to hold the newborn child. Bob stayed with Lucy in the bedroom, holding her hand and using his other to cradle his wife's clammy face. The birth had not been as rough on Lucy as they had feared, yet they knew the danger for any child born to a mother who had been ill during the carriage.

Aurelia took a pair of shears she'd boiled in water and cut the cord. She held the baby up for the two of them to see. "Girl child," she said.

Lucy smiled. Bob took a washcloth and wiped his wife's forehead. "A girl," he said, as though he wasn't sure if she had been listening. To Aurelia he said, "Give her a look over and bring her back to us."

Aurelia took the child to the basin on the porch. Night came in. She washed the film and blood from the infant's body. She swaddled the child and held her up to look her over. The child, not yet named, had neither gasped nor cried but with a smack began to breathe. The baby's skin had a pinkish-gray cast about it, but she was quiet and blinked with drowsy contentment in the darkness of Aurelia's arms. The warm midsummer air surrounded them both. Aurelia's young son, Rawls, stood watching his mother rock the child from the yard as marbled moonlight fell through the expanse of the sycamore tree's darkening crown. Aurelia saw that the child's eyes were cloudy with cataracts. The pupils a swirl of the lightest gray at the center of dark, gold-flecked irises. She was sure the child was blind, and at that moment she began to tell the girl in a voice, one that sounded very much like singing, that it would be a hard life, that tomorrow would be a hard day, as would the day after and the day after that. But as she cradled her she saw the girl's strange eyes moving toward points of light; the lamp burning with a quiet hiss, lightning bugs flickering in the yard, and what stars that could be seen from Chesterfield County assembled in the heavens.

The first years of her life, or the times from those years that held their shapes firmly enough to be recalled in later ones, were simple. Her father's mule skinning made enough money to give them a comfortable life. Their home on the road between the coalfields and the river was modest but respectable. Aurelia attended to her dutifully. Emily became accustomed to Rawls's presence even though she thought him peculiar. One summer he wove himself a hat out of green tobacco leaves and she told him he was silly for not wearing a proper hat. Sometimes she'd watch him brush the mules' coats to such a sleekness that they seemed carved from polished stone. At dusk he'd often take a homemade cane pole and cast it toward the heavens until bats whooshed down like rain from the blue-black sky. She did not know how old he was except that he was leaving boyhood. When she asked him he said, "I'm old enough, Miss Emily," and slinked away.

When she was five years old her father had let her keep a runt bird-dog whelp she'd found in a ditch. She named her Champion. Rawls did not care for the dog. He thought she was unruly and spoiled, though Master Reid had taught her some basic commands. Rawls's meekness toward Champion gave Emily fits of laughter. By the time she was eight she'd invented a game for the three of them to play. She'd tie the birder to the sycamore and tease her mercilessly, pulling the bitch's ears and rapping her snout with a folded fan until she yelped and spun herself into a knot. When the dog finally quivered submissively she'd unravel the rope and bark out a command she'd learned while watching her father train the dog. And Rawls would run as best he could to get away, sometimes climbing up a near tree or onto the roof of the mule pen or, when he was truly stricken by fear, toward the big house, calling for his mother all the way. One afternoon Bob returned home early and saw Emily at this game, the teenage Rawls balancing in terror on a tall fence post, and he beat her savagely with his belt right out in the yard. He kicked the dog away from its pacing under the fence and helped Rawls down. "Gosh dang it, Emily," he said, "you're gonna make this boy a runner again. Now leave him be so he can get about my business!"

Bob went in the house and slammed the door behind him. Emily wept a puddle under the tree. Rawls turned to see the dog looking at him with her brown head curiously cocked to one side. The frightened yellow eyes told him she had been running away, not toward, the whole time. Rawls looked over at the girl sprawled out and wailing in the grass and envied her. Her pain in that moment was real pain, no different in expression from his own. He knew the way one's chest got bound up, how a strange heat came to the cheeks and boiled over into tears of rage and frustration. The difference, though, was in source and scope. While hers came from a rare remonstration by her father, his was inscrutable and vast. She would weep in the yard for an hour at most, then skulk back to her father's forgiving kisses. His was forever married to all the memories he had and joined again to every new memory he made. Tomorrow she would leave the house, and pain would be as incomprehensible to the girl's mind as the map of a foreign country in a schoolbook. He had found no boundary to his own.

When the girl recovered she straightened out her skirts and dusted them off. She looked at Rawls and wiped the tears from her cheeks with the backs of her hands. "It's only a game," she said. She turned toward a field waving golden in the white sun beyond the mule pen. He watched her go, silently. And he determined in that moment to find something that would not be subject to the strange laws of the borderless world in which he lived. Something he could claim that they could not. Anything they could not take from him. And he began to run in the nights again, as in his childhood, in search of it.

Several winters passed without incident for Rawls. Some snowless, others so bleak he could not distinguish between the earth and sky for all the snow that seemed to fall between the two. He ventured out at night and was not caught. He had no destination other than the one he circled unconsciously: a notion of being engaged in a desperate search. He had no respect for white folks anymore, and very rarely fear, but he sometimes pitied them, allowing himself pity only because he had once heard a traveling preacher say that pity was the cruelest feeling one could have toward another.

By 1860 he was in charge of most of the freight Bob Reid's mules pulled down the narrow-gauge tracks toward Richmond. He might oversee the shipment of tons of bituminous coal out of the Midlothian mines, or great hogsheads of tobacco cropped from endless fields late in the summer, and he was trusted throughout the county to make sure every single cured leaf and every fat black lump of coal got to market in as good a state as when they were put onto his carts.

On account of his high standing in the community as both a reliable and efficient part of the local economy, Bob gave Rawls a pass, dawn to dusk, that was essentially without any other restrictions. When there was no harvest, and as that hard coal out of Pennsylvania slowly dropped the value of the dull local brittle, Rawls could be seen at leisure on one of Bob's ponies, always the same one, a brindle named Dorothea, with a big cedar-handled tobacco knife tucked into his britches, and a dirty fur felt hat on his head tipped back to near upright.

He'd pass by people at Levallois Crossing, or farmers on the ferry road, and reach high up toward the crown of his hat, saying "Afternoon" to whomever he'd come across. A gentle ribbing would then ensue. A kind of inside joke that nobody got left out of. "You best be carrying that pass, Rawls," they'd smilingly chide. And he'd pat his left breast and answer back, "Course you know I do." And Rawls would then touch his hat again, spur on his pony, and check sometimes three and four times that the pass was truly there.

Near evening, when circumstances provided, he'd almost always end up near the ferry landing. The bateau man was a surly old dark-skinned hillbilly named Spanish Jim, and being equally ambivalent toward all, he never minded if Rawls stripped off his clothes and dove from the big bluestem grass into water as brown and still as a medicinal bottle. At that hour, with the sun going down in the break in the trees above the curling river, and the grasshopper sparrows' trill song darting through the meadow, Rawls managed to fall into a state resembling contentment.

As the water ran over his body, he'd often recall his first trip down to the river as a boy. He'd been about six years old, not quite two years before he stood in the dooryard and watched his mother rock the strange girl who would so influence the rest of his life. At that time, they had just been sold to Bob Reid; his mother to tend to the ailing Lucy Reid, Rawls to become a muleteer, though he did not know what that was when he was told it was the thing he was going to become.

His previous owner had taken them on a long trip southwest down a road choked with dust and then across the river on the bateau. The ferryman looked at Rawls blankly as he pushed the long straight pole and shook his head ever so slightly. Rawls stared back, wondering if he was a black man or a white man. "No man steps into the same river twice, boy," said Spanish Jim, surprising Rawls. "You think on that awhile. That's old wisdom." When they arrived at the far shore Rawls remembered standing sheepishly and unsteadily on his barely healed feet during the transaction. His first owner saying, "Dammit, Bob. You're getting a hell of a deal here. Woman's good in the house. Good with children. But the young one's just all around impertinent. Too sharp for his own good."

"He's a runner, you say?"

"Was. Won't be no more. Had to dock his toes. Boy couldn't get out of sight in a day now. But between his bellyaching and Aurelia's wailing over top, don't neither of 'em get shit done. Almost feel bad making you pay."

"But not that bad."

"No. I reckon not. But if you can get 'em right you're getting a hell of a deal."

The years between then and now had pressed forward dully and relentlessly like a river downstream from a terrible storm. But Rawls's nighttime wanderings were beginning to fill him with a curious joy despite their inherent danger. He did not know if he would find the thing that could not be taken from him, but he felt that it was close. He sat waiting in their small cabin back in the woods behind the mule pen. Aurelia slept soundly in a bed he'd made for her out of rope and straw and pieces of driftwood for the posts. He stuck his head out the window. The moon waned to its last quarter. Rawls put on his moccasins and waited for his mother to begin snoring. He hoped that night to see a girl named Nurse again. She lived an hour's walk west on a thousand-acre soybean farm that skirted the river just across the Chesterfield line into eastern Powhatan County. A week before, he had taken the mules to the soybean farm to retrieve a load of cargo bound for the river. The voices in the fields all sang "Steal Away to Jesus," and the eyes in the field all looked toward a ribbon of loblolly pine that stood at the boundary between three plantations.

He found those same voices at their prayer meeting that night, gathered in a glade they'd cut into the dense pinewoods. Rawls never had much use for God, and as they sang he sat silently and his mind wandered. He thought of lightning he'd seen flashing in a recent storm. How little danger there was unless you were right out under it. And yet, like the mules under the stable roof that brayed at the thunderclaps, it caused everyone to tremble. Why fear that which would come or not regardless of your fear? he wondered. The brim of his hat tilted over his face like a veil, and in the deepest shadow of the night he closed his eyes. Like a blind man, he reconstructed the world as he imagined it could be. And it occurred to him that there were few things he was truly afraid of anymore.

He noticed the girl that night among the pines. She was about his age, he'd guessed, lingering motionless at the edge of the firelight. She wore a calico wrap fixed atop her head in an impossibly complex arrangement. Small orange petals spread across a field of the darkest blue one might find in the evening sky, which seemed to Rawls to put all the true colors of the world to shame. She was calm in her solitude but not withdrawn, as if her mere presence was equally participatory to the human sound and motion that swirled around her. He smiled at her. Put up his hand in a still wave of greeting.

He saw her again the night he left Aurelia sleeping under the last quarter of the moon and on many nights after they would meet in that patch of pines, sitting off on their own a little apart from the prayer meeting. Some nights they would have the woods to themselves and it would seem the whole world had shrunk down to a few acres of loblolly beneath the breezy midnight stars. He learned they called her Nurse on account of her wet-nursing her master's babies, all nine of which would go on to reach adulthood. "You don't want to get a proper name?" he asked her. To which she replied that she had her letters and had come to read about other women with her name and that it suited her just fine. "And, Rawls," she said, "where'd you get that name?"

"Don't know."

Along with her letters she had learned a fair bit of doctoring. Not just midwifery, in which she was peerless even at that age, but also the mending of bones and cuts and the treatment of all manner of interior afflictions which she'd gathered by tending to her owner's mules and horses. One night they took a walk together and before they'd gone far she pulled at Rawls's elbow to stop him. "Why do you have a gait like a hobbled dog?"

They were near a clearing then, and the clearing was dotted with cedar as it sloped toward a pond and creek that fed the river. They sat down in a spot of low grass and he took off his hand-me-down moccasins. Nurse looked down at his feet. The moon was out, but clouds passed beneath it, turning the gold grass white and the cedars into thin shadows. Rawls was missing the big toe on both of his feet. The soles were rough and calloused and reached up toward the uneven scarring where the toes had been. "Runner," he said.

"Who done this to you?"

"Old man who owned us before."

"Does it still pain you?"

Rawls whistled and smiled. "Not like it once did. I get sore a bit from walking hinky. The old man did it hisself. He caught me sneaking past the big house and knocked me on my backside. Dragged me to a snake fence, tied my feet to the top rail, stood on my shoulders, and gave 'em a whack with a hatchet."

Nurse sighed and shook her head. "What were you running for?"

"You got to ask? I was running to get gone."

They had been still and quiet long enough that the common noises of the night returned. The nightjar's solemn whistle. A fox scream in the distance. The world painted in shades of gray and lit solely by reflection.

"It hurt like hell at the time," said Rawls. "I was such a little feller he had to lift me off the ground partways to get my feet tied to the rail. Left me hanging upside down till the next day."

Nurse reached out and touched his ankle. Massaged up toward his calf and down again. "But you had your momma with you."

"Don't preach."

"And now?" Nurse asked. "You ain't never worried she'll catch what's meant for you?"

"Not likely. Master Bob don't have the stomach for it. He puts on like he does sometimes, just for show. But I see these white folks coming. They never see me, but I can figure 'em pretty good now. 'Sides, my momma knows my nature. And she knows any one of us might catch what's meant for another."

"You wouldn't miss her if something happened?" Nurse asked.

"Course I would." He paused, searching for what seemed like an impossible arrangement of words. He said, "I been with her my whole life and I already miss her. I missed her that whole time. I'm missing her right at this moment."

"I never had my momma with me that I recall. Don't know her name. Don't know if I favor her."

"I ain't saying it's the same, but I missed your momma before I heard you say that. Missed her like my own. Missed her like I'm missing you right now."

He lay out in the grass and propped himself up on his elbows. He heard the creek go by and followed it in his mind. Down into the James. Past the fall line. Past the docks and beyond the place of sighs at Lumpkin's slave jail. Out into wide water. Brackish and flat and a mile across. Out into the bay until its blue chop became the ocean, where it left behind the cypresses and cattails, and the land remained only as a misremembered dream.

"I understand, Rawls. I do. And I miss you, too."

Nurse kissed him. Pushed his body deep into the grass. The woods grew quiet again on their behalf. Rawls decided he loved Nurse. And that perhaps his love for her was the thing that could not be taken from him. But he would not see her again for a good long while.

In the days and nights that followed his last meeting with Nurse, he waited for her in the loblolly stand. He waited every night for a month, but she did not come. He'd heard the prayer meetings were outlawed by Nurse's master, that some incident at the soybean plantation caused the man to go mad. Talk that he had shut off his little kingdom from the rest of the world abounded. Rawls did not dare cross its border at first. Instead he spent his days working tirelessly for Mr. Bob, chopping at wood, mending far fences, only to again sneak out of his mother's cabin at night. He fell into a fevered state. He moved through nights so dark he'd have sworn he'd been struck blind. On others he ran as best he could between degrees of deeper shadow cast by the bright moon. His mind trembled with exhaustion. Nurse filled his thoughts until the boundaries between dream and wakefulness dissolved. The noise of his strange gait through the understory became a regularity in the dark woods.

He held out hope that she'd been sold nearby. He was rushed out of slave quarters on plantations from the river damn near down to Amelia County in his search for her, the whispers thrown behind him saying, "Get back where you belong before you get somebody dead!" And still he searched. He searched until he wondered if he himself might not be dead, if he had not fallen under some curse or conjuration through which Nurse had been but a spirit devised to torture him with her abandonment. He returned to places he had been before, now covered in snow, and again in spring as the dead nettle pushed its purple flowers out into the cool morning air.

At last he broke. He gathered his strength against rumor and uncertainty and finally made his way west toward whatever might await him beyond the patch of pines. He snuck up on an old man curled in his blanket on the floor of a cabin just within the boundary of the soybean plantation. Torches bobbed at the edges of the wide fields. Rawls stuck his head through the unglazed window and saw white hair and a white beard and heard the steady breath of sleep. He went through the front door and knelt in the hard-packed dirt next to the old man. With one hand Rawls gently covered the old man's mouth. The breath was warm and it filled his cupped palm. The old man's hands were tucked up under his beard where they held the patchwork blanket beneath his chin. Rawls clasped his other hand around the old man's knuckles and began to gently wake him, whispering, "Granddad. Old Granddad."

The old man woke with a start. He opened his rheumy eyes and rubbed at them, saying, "Who is this here? What do you want? My time come?" The old man sat up and looked Rawls over. "You ain't no apparition. What are you doing in my cabin?"

"I've been searching after Nurse, Granddad. You know her? Prettiest girl you ever seen. Most times wore a kind of blue calico wrap over her hair."

"I hardly know pretty these days, son," he said. Granddad leaned over to a small cedar box, pulled out a tallow candle and a match, and lit it. "What you hunting her for anyhow?"

Rawls could see up and down the old man's arms. They were lined with mark after mark of whip and brine, a topography of the passage of time and pain one on top of the other, a map in miniature of ridgeline and ravine going up into his shirtsleeves in an uninterrupted pattern.

"I need her," Rawls said.

"You aim to do her harm?"

"Naw, Granddad," he said. "I love her."

The old man looked disappointed. "No place for love in this world, son."

"I'll make a place. Don't you worry. Where is she?"

"This world's gonna break your damn heart, boy."

"It's been broke already."

The old man sighed. "I seen her sent off 'cross the river.

I heard she gone to Lumpkin's Jail. Gone straight to the Devil's Half Acre."

The thought of the place knocked him back. "It ain't true," Rawls said angrily. He felt his pulse throbbing under his eyes, wanted to grab out for something to steady him, but there was just the old man's shoulder, which flagged and trembled under his weight. "It ain't true," he said again.

The old man reached out and grabbed both of Rawls's hands, holding them gently but firmly as he told him how his mistress had been thrown from her horse the previous fall, just before the prayer meetings were shut down, and that she was found by Nurse laid out under a post oak with her arms and legs looking crooked as the tree's tangle of limbs above her. The horse that threw her stamping nearby through the orange blaze of fallen leaves. Its snorting and the wind the only sounds besides Nurse hollering for help. Nurse tended to her night and day. Her master even kept the doctor away, so much did he trust Nurse with his wife's care. But a week later mistress died, and master caught a hatred for Nurse on account of her not saving his wife, and he took to beating her for sport, day after day and week after week. It got so bad that the other slaves begged him to show Nurse mercy, till some of them started to get beatings of their own when they did. They did not see her anymore as winter came. They no longer heard her cry out at night. It was assumed that Nurse was dead. Not long after, in the depth of winter, the river froze solid. Their master took it as a bad omen and sold Nurse off to Robert Lumpkin, thinking her absence would rid him of his tribulations. But his hatred for her burned still. And while he had been unable to cleanse his thoughts of Nurse, his hatred had been transformed into a pleasurable speculation in which he would imagine Nurse's life as it might be at Lumpkin's Jail, where the fire of hatred and cruelty never so much as flagged to ember. The last the old man saw of Nurse was her lying motionless in the back of a cart as one of the drivers took the cart gingerly onto the ice, and the wheels of the cart rolled smoothly across. "Son," he said to Rawls, "that girl is gone. If she ain't sold down the river yet, I doubt she'd know you if you found her."

On that same night in the early spring of 1861, Emily Reid, now almost fourteen years old, was troubled by dreams. She'd tossed in her quilt since nightfall, but there had been nothing overtly terrifying in her visions that she could recall on waking. No monsters. No ghosts. Just one scene over and over, clearer than any vision her cloudy eyes would allow her during the day, a dream in which she stood in a sun-splashed upland field watching Champion's ticked coat of brown and white dart in and out of the tall grass as the mechanical whir of what seemed to be a million cicadas drummed the air.

When she woke she paced her room. She put a candle on her windowsill and looked out. Champion was awake under the big sycamore in the yard. The dog had her haunches up behind her and began to bark, first in a series of low and incomplete grumbles, then finally letting go full throated until Emily worried her agitation might break the glass in the

windows. She blew out the candle, shuffled quietly downstairs, and went into the yard. "Hush, girl," she said. The
moon was on the wane but still bright and the dog bounded
crazily at the end of the rope they leashed her with at night.
"Hush, Champion. Please, girl. You're gonna wake the dead
out here."

By then her parents were roused by the commotion. Her
mother hollered at Emily from her window to get inside
while Bob sat on the porch and put his boots on.

"You hear your mother calling you, girl? It's past midnight."

"But Champion's all riled up, Papa."

Bob looked to the edge of the woods that seemed to
house the source of Champion's discontentment. No lights
to be seen from Aurelia's cabin deeper in the trees behind
the mule pen. He took the rope and lifted its loop off the
post it had been tied to. He seemed to forget about Emily
and let the dog off her leash.

She bounded out into the woods. When they caught up
to her a few minutes later she was stopped, almost pointing,
but not quite, into a clearing where the Reids' property
abutted Beauvais Plantation. Aurelia came up behind them.
Rawls did not know it, but whenever he left the cabin at
night, Aurelia woke and nervously waited for his return.

She hoped to intervene. "Please, Master Reid, he's just
a boy."

Bob looked at Emily. Her strange eyes luminous in the
shadows cinched like baling twine around the woods. Bob
had raised his daughter no different than if she'd been a son.

She would be his only child, as the doctors said with certainty that Lucy's womb was shot, and so his expectations of her were different than if she'd been some other man's daughter. "Listen close," he said to Emily. "Go get my pistol and shotgun."

Aurelia wailed feebly. "Master Reid, why do you need your guns? He probably just gone off to see this young thing he got an affinity for."

"Emily, go," he said. And then to Aurelia, punctuating his annoyance with a jab at the tender flesh where Aurelia's collarbones met, "I don't give a dusty fuck why he ran off, Aurelia. And you can thank John Brown and the rest of abolitiondom for me taking my guns. Now go up to the house with Miss Lucy till I get this sorted." He paused, and said begrudgingly as he turned away from her, "I don't aim to harm him if he'll let me not."

TWO

ON THE LAST Monday morning of his life, George Seldom took a bath, shaved with a new razor bought from Levy's store the day before, dressed in jeans, a denim shirt, and a ratty buckskin coat he'd had for as long as he could remember. By 9:00 a.m. he'd made a cup of coffee and found himself on his front porch staring into an abyss.

A week earlier, on an unusually hot day in June of 1956, a crew of surveyors from the Richmond-Petersburg Turnpike Authority joined a crew of workers from the State Highway Department at the intersection of St. Peter and Baker Streets in the Jackson Ward neighborhood of Richmond, Virginia. A group of dignitaries and press walked north up St. Peter Street to join them. Their collective presence, it was noted by many of the local residents watching this spectacle take place, had increased the number of white folks in the neighborhood by a rather significant margin. When the men met at the intersection they shook hands and posed for pictures. A local assemblyman and member of Senator Harry Flood Byrd's organization made a great show of swinging a ceremonial pickax into the dirt street where the excavations were to begin.

Construction commenced on that section of the interstate highway through Richmond by pulling the old roads up, brick by brick where there was brick, one cobblestone at a time where there was cobble, and shovelful after shovelful of dirt everywhere else. And then they'd bring the houses down, houses that for a long time had kept the disappearing streets in shadow. Some of George's neighbors lined the sidewalks, crossing their arms and grieving for the demolition of the last of those beautiful old Federal houses, which it seemed still stood only out of sheer orneriness until the cranes dropped heavily onto their metal roofs, collapsing them forever. From time to time he could see the rise and fall of the yellow jaws of the excavator when it appeared above the lip of the void to leave yet another piece of the past in a haphazard heap. Brick, wood, and cobble intermixed in a half-dozen piles. There had once been a row of houses opposite his own, a block to the east of where the excavations had begun, and now, in their place, only the air remained. His eyesight, not what it once was, could still make out a pattern on the far wall of the excavated earth: first soil, then clay, then down into the rotten rock into which they'd cut and dug, and farther down the sparkle of some firmer stone where the morning sun reached in and cast out the last of the early shadows.

Beyond the scar, into which a mixer had begun depositing a steady stream of aggregate and water, George watched a group of children playing in the abandoned bed of a rusted-out Ford truck. He could hear their voices, shrill and joyful, as they called out to stake their claim to the prize, ownership of the view of the assembled workers that the rusted roofline of the truck provided, and finally one boy, about ten years old, his shirtless chest puffed out and black as iron, swept away his adversaries with a beat-up push broom, declared his victory and dominion over this small stretch of the world in words that lost their shape and form by the time they got to George, but not their meaning.

He sat down on the bench in front of his parlor window and noticed that the newest of the patches on his coat had lost its stitching. It took a good long while for leather to wear out, he thought, this skin like any other, and he made a note to walk over to Levy's store to get a needle and thread to mend it. As he surveyed the scene before him, the shuffle and hum of what he thought were the last of the changes he might see, he decided that today would be as good a day as any other. He'd had a long life, some-where in the neighborhood of ninety years, he guessed, and full enough of the things he thought would qualify to make it good. He'd been married twice, in love once, and, though childless from both, could say with certainty that he had had a place in this world, despite the fact that the ground we use to mark those places always seems to shift beneath us.

Around noon on that day in June, George walked the three blocks over to Mr. Levy's store on Brook and Marshall. He was surprised to see that not much more than the counter remained inside. The balance of the inventory sat in orderly stacks on the herringbone brick of the sidewalk, through which a few yellow dandelions had made their way, though the bell still dinged reliably as George opened the door and went inside. Mr. Levy looked up from the counter at its sound and walked around to greet him.

"George, my friend. You are looking well today," he said as he reached out to shake his hand. Henry Levy was middle aged, with a youthful energy well suited to his profession. He was the third Henry Levy to have operated Levy's grocery. The first was his grandfather, who opened it after a not unreasonably distinguished period of service with the Quartermaster Corps of the Confederate Army of Tennessee. George shook his hand and said, "You looking well, your own self, Mr. Levy, if you don't mind my saying." He smiled and led George to a parlor chair near the storefront windows and asked him if he'd care for something to drink. George waved him off wordlessly and took in the emptiness of the shop that had, over time, become a fixture of the neighborhood and a common piece of his own world. "So, y'all'll be leaving, too, I guess?"

"Well, George," Mr. Levy said, "Route One just isn't going to carry people the way it used to now." His speech was a mixture of Philadelphia schools and the Tidewater South, accented by the Hebrew his father had made sure he learned at temple. It was a drawl nearly, but not quite, canceled out by the ancient tongue he carried with him despite its loneliness in the land in which his family had finally settled. "We're moving to a place across the river."

"All the way out to the counties?" George asked, with more than a little surprise.

"You know we used to get people stopping in from as far as Florida?" said Levy.

"Maine, too, I think I've heard you say."

"Yes. Maine, too. Canada. Philadelphia. Now...?" He made a sound like paper tearing and moved his hands in an accompanying theatricality. "A wound as deep as the sea."

Maine to Florida, thought George. North to south, a road built and cultivated through commerce and commiseration.

"Now Eisenhower wants to build roads big enough for bombers to land on. For when the Russians come, I reckon."

"Is that a fact?" asked George.

A sun shower began pelting the window in bands of light and rain. "I only know what the *Times Dispatch* says are the facts," he said, raising his hands in mocking jest.

George laughed and looked out the window. He imagined the great silver belly of a bomber, big as the sky, circling the corbeled facades and wrought-iron gates of Jackson Ward. Then circling wider over the statues of the white folks' southern saints on Monument Avenue, over the cemetery on the hill, over all those poor slaves buried behind Main Street Station where Lumpkin would toss their bodies out like garbage when they'd die in his jail, over the river, over the South, the United States, and the whole damn world. "Well, Mr. Levy, I guess if he's gonna send them planes up, which he's surely gonna do, he's damn sure gonna give 'em somewhere to land."

The rain put a pause on that stretch of the interstate's

construction for the day. Several men jogged past the store-front in hard hats, splashing their Red Wings through the newly formed puddles, laughing very much like the children George had seen playing in the empty lot before. The oldest worker's belly shook like a sack of discarded cats as he jogged, and as he splashed into a puddle before they reached Broad Street, he shouted gleefully, "Maybe if we're lucky all these niggers'll drown!"

George turned toward Mr. Levy slowly and deliberately, not with anger but curiosity. Mr. Levy had turned away and was arranging a stack of papers on the counter. George could not articulate his feelings in that moment exactly, but it seemed to him that Mr. Levy had not turned away in shame, not quite, but rather had turned away in an effort to avoid the shame he knew was floating unclaimed in the front room of his shop.

The quiet was interrupted by the sound of a flatbed truck pulling up into the loading zone out front on Marshall Street. Tarps ruffled back from their anchors. George had forgotten why he'd come. It was not the first time. He some-times felt as if time were speeding up like a car with a stuck gas pedal, and though he had long since set aside the self-pity that can accompany the certainty that one's death is closer than one's birth, he remained filled with frustra-tion. He would have the clarity of an ending, had even set aside six hundred dollars for Crawley's Funeral Home on St. James to do him up right and lay him down next to his second wife, Leona, in the second of two plots at Oakwood Cemetery he'd bought for them when they were flush. The city had surrendered all but the small Confederate section to the encroaching forest in the years since, and though he visited her grave quite a bit just after she'd passed, over time he could not think of much to say to her, nor did he have much faith she would have heard him if he did. He doubted he'd be buried there when the time came anyway, as he figured it would take six men a month of digging to clear out enough of the creeping ivy to find the dirt in which to lay him down.

As to his beginning, he knew nothing. That part of him had been a void so long it had taken shape around its edges. How was it that he'd found himself as a small boy, filthy with dust, waiting alone on the porch of a spinster's house at the edge of the Lumber River in North Carolina with nothing but his name, the clothes he wore, and a hurriedly inscribed note that said *Look after me. I now belong to you.* Before this, there was nothing, perhaps a name some days. No, not a name, someone calling for a nurse in the farthest reaches of his memory. So far back it isn't even a memory but a story he imagines listening to, of which he can recall neither the tale nor the teller, hopeful that at some point in the past the truth had a chance of getting told.

He woke to Henry Levy the fourth calling to him, gently shaking his shoulders. "George. George. You've nodded off." Mr. Levy's only son and heir stood over him. He was handsome, about twenty years old, and tanned as dark as George from his weekend train rides down to Virginia Beach. His hair was cut close like a soldier's. "Are you all right, George?" he asked.

"I'm fine, son. Fine. Just got to reminiscing. Saps my strength these days."

"Aw, hell," the younger Henry said, "seems like you got plenty of life left in you, old-timer."

He had his father's cultivated warmth. It would serve him in good stead over the years. He and his father would go on to open another grocery store in Forest Hill, and then another out near Midlothian, then leverage those into a number of A&Ps with which they had even greater success.

"Henry, my young friend," George said, "didn't anybody ever tell you that seems ain't is?"

Mr. Levy wrote out an address on a piece of paper and gave it to George. "The new shop," he said. "Come see us." And then, "Will you stay in the city? I know some folks are taking the city up on that municipal housing between here and Northside. Gilpin Court? Sounds kind of nice, has sort of a regal air to it."

"No," George answered. "I've been in my own house too long to start over. I thought they'd be taking me out feetfirst before long, but now, I don't know. It's one of the ones getting torn down. Got a little money for it from 'em, but a damn sight less than it's worth." He paused and then said, "You know, Mr. Levy, it occurs to me that y'all might be the last white folks in the neighborhood."

Henry the younger paused in the doorway at this comment and turning back toward the older man said, "Don't worry, George. We might be white folks here in the ward, but we've lived in this town long enough to know that the

Levys will be Jews again by the time we hit the Nickel Bridge and cross that river."

A few hours later George sat in Broad Street Station's colored waiting room. When he had first come to Richmond in the teens, he had watched mule teams pull stumps from the edges of the land on which the station had been built. A marble hall raised up out of the manure stink of the abandoned fairgrounds' stockyard. And now through the frosted glass of the waiting room he could hear the jostle and buzz of travelers in the marble rotunda, here and there snippets of a tour: "The man who made the Jefferson Memorial...noble rooms...a hierarchy of spaces...the synthesis of all the highly mannered styles."

He had not taken much from the house he'd left behind; a few changes of clothes, a copy of *The Negro Travelers' Green Book*, another book he'd been given as a gift by Mr. Levy's late father, and a lovely little knife with a handle of elk antler that he'd owned as long as he could remember. In his shirt pocket he had a one-way ticket for the 1:55 *Everglades* of the Atlantic Coast Line that would put him off near Fayetteville that evening, not far from where his childhood memories began. He thought of the dust of North Carolina roads, high white light in summer falling through a trellis of leaning hardwood and plumb-straight pine, the black water of the motionless Lumber River. How cool it was to swim in once. And how bitter the tannins still sometimes tasted in his mouth.

He bought a copy of the *News Leader*, looked at his watch, and sat back down on the wooden bench next to his suitcase. Senator Harry Flood Byrd's smiling face looked back at him from its perch next to a gushing editorial. "Massive Resistance" read the headline. He folded up the broadsheet with a sigh and deposited it into a trash can just as the conductor called for boarding to begin.

The train rolled over the James River Railway Bridge's gray arches in the angled light of the afternoon sun. The bridge had always seemed monumental to him at a distance. George could see boulders and white water. Slender islands covered with trees skirted the edges of the river's main channel. The illusion of a wilderness remained. He thought, for a moment, that if he had his life to live again he would do it in a wild place. Montana. The solitude of the Andes he had once seen in a discarded issue of *National Geographic* as a boy. Trouble on his own terms. But he knew this kind of thinking was a fantasy. The trouble he was born with was not the kind that can be locked away in a cedar chest and left behind. And he also knew that the terms the world lays out for us are not negotiable.

He woke up as the train crossed another nameless watershed near the North Carolina border. The surface flat as paper. He did not expect answers more complete or satisfying than those he'd already been given. Maybe another question would come to mind. But he felt that all the questions people ask themselves are simply variations on "why." *Why me? Why her? Why now?* He wondered if the world had been kind to him. It would take everything from him eventually, but it seemed to him that it would not take anything that had not belonged to the world first.

He'd noticed a young marine board the train back in Petersburg. As the evening progressed George saw that they were the only ones left in the car. The marine walked down the aisle toward George and asked, "May I join you, sir?"

"Of course, son. You sit right down." George was in his seventies before he gave up the bristling resentment he'd previously felt toward the concern the young often have for the old. He didn't mind it now. It was one small purpose he felt that he could still provide: from time to time putting his remaining pride aside so one human being could be useful to another. The boy, for most men in the world now seemed so much like boys to George, wore his green uniform smartly. Gold bars shined from his collar. A shield with wings above a few ribbons.

George asked him if he had kin in Petersburg.

"I did, but not anymore. We laid my grandmother to rest. I'm heading back to Cherry Point."

"Where the rest of your people?" asked George.

"Kansas. Topeka."

"Kansas?" George said, whistling. "Can't say I ever made it there. What do you do in the service, son?" he asked.

"I'm an aviator, sir."

"A what now?"

"I fly airplanes."

The day before seemed a thousand years ago to George; the time before airplanes closer to Adam than to now. Fifty-some-odd years had passed since the Wrights flung their contraption off the dunes of Kill Devil Hills and ever so briefly into the sky. He'd been told about it not long after the unprecedented event by an itinerant worker named Huggins who'd come into the logging camp in the Great Dismal Swamp, the place that had been the closest thing to a home George would know for many years. Midwinter snow hung in the cypress branches. The foreman called a pause in the action. "Got a new rube here, boys, name of Huggins. Show him how we do things and don't let him get hisself killed just yet." A teenage boy strolled up and said, "Which of y'all Seldom? I'm supposed to be bucker to his faller."

The boy could not contain himself. George had to remind him to go slow and pay attention, unless he wanted to get thumped stone dead before supper. They'd left a dozen men in the canals and black swamp water over the time George had worked there. He supposed whoever owned the operation, a detail he did not know, might figure that the ten thousand acres they'd clear-cut by then was a good return on that investment. And when he'd take the trail out to Lake Drummond, it seemed that the result of all their falling was to bring the broad lake near to level with the land, to have created a disconcerting relationship between earth and sky and water. The long scar of an open field where the swamp drained into the lake, bare but for a tangle of stumps on which, from time to time, an eagle might come to rest.

But the boy threw himself into talk and work, so much so that his voice began to register to George's hearing as just another version of the hum and gurgle that accompanied their labor. Chattering beneath the drag of the mule sleds. Buzzing with the saws' teeth as they cut logs to length.

Shouting with the drumbeat of axes into bark. As they sat at supper near camp where the long dirt road, now dusted with snow, paralleled the canal, Huggins told George why he'd come.

"It's progress I'm after, Mr. Seldom. Where else can I look up and see what I've accomplished at the end of the day, clear as this place here?"

And it was true, in a way, what the boy said. The gaps in the drowned forest were an indisputable record that they made more so every day.

George waited for Huggins to take a breath, then said, "Feller tells me a while back, when I first got put on, that most of these woods end up as shingles on rich folks' summerhouses in New England. Mansions with their doors right up to the edge of the sea. And he tells me he gets a hankering to see 'em. This is back in ninety, maybe ninety-one. So he saves his pennies until he's fixed for a train ticket to a place called Provincetown. And when he gets up there the damn place is lousy with cedar shake. He tells me they look right pretty, but they got to strip them off and put up new ones all the time on account of all the salt and sand and wind and whatnot. Water ain't a problem, but they ain't accounted for the rest. So, when he comes back down he gets to figuring how much clear-cut goes for one house, and these are right big houses now, and I ain't never seen a sadder picture of a man. Also he tells me, goes into a tavern one night and gets to talking with this fancy joker got him a hotel right up there near the harbor, and this hotel got cedar and white cypress all over. And when this feller finds out my pal's on a logging outfit, he sighs and says what a sin it is we doin' to God's creation. Now ain't that just some shit?"

"A sign of the times is what I'd call it."

"A sign of the times? Hug, you ain't old enough to know 'em when you see 'em," said George.

"Well, you might be right," Huggins replied. "But I was just down on the Outer Banks a few weeks past and I seen two fellers out of Ohio put themselves up into the sky. Now tell me that ain't some kind of augury."

To hear Huggins tell it, the scene was one of singular beauty, of a kind that George could hardly comprehend and by which he was slightly terrified. He could only respond to the tale by infrequently offering stuttering questions, which might have seemed like rebuttals to passersby but for the timbre of his voice. "In the sky, you say? How far? Tell the truth now, Huggins. I ain't as dumb as you think."

"Honest Injun," said Hug.

George eyed him curiously, then broke into laughter. "You almost had me there."

"God as my witness, George."

"I don't believe it. You mean to tell me man can fly?"

And yes, that is what he meant to say. George could scarcely imagine it. Huggins's voice persisted in the background as he saw sand and water rippling out forever, indistinguishable in his colorless dream. It could have been the surface of the moon from which this strange machine sputtered. The plane drifted just above the sands, its white muslin wings nearly glancing the dunes, as if the dunes and nearby sea themselves unfurled the wings as flags, forever ceding their formerly terrestrial possession of mankind.

There was something irreconcilable to George about this knowledge. For days after he swung his ax in a desperate frenzy, twisting like a spun top until his legs sank into the black water of the swamp up to his knees, until the trees crashed down one by one into the water. He would look upward as the winter quiet of the swamp returned, searching the void left in the canopy for a white dot in transit across the small circle of sky that he'd helped make. He did not expect to see the plane, of course. Truthfully, he did not know what he hoped to see, but he knew he had not seen it. And he began to doubt he ever would.

George fell into a depression not long after giving up his search of the skies above Great Dismal. And when Huggins was killed by the unexpected trajectory of the fall of a giant Atlantic white in the first week of February 1904, the boy's death took its place among all the unanswerable questions from his life. He had not been the faller on that one, having been laid out by a fever, and he was lying in his tent when the team came back in moody silence, the first time they had done so since before Huggins had arrived. Perhaps the rest of the crew anticipated that he would feel responsible for having been absent when the boy was struck, so they assured him there was nothing he or anybody else could have done to stop it. "Goddamn tree barber-chaired on him like you wouldn't believe, George," they said. And so to close the subject they agreed that it had been overdue, that the swamp had not been paid for what she had given up in a good long while.

George thought of Huggins often after the boy's death. Logrolling in the icy water of the Dismal Swamp Canal. The boy's freckled face beaming carelessly, eyes closed, as he spun a length of timber under the heels of his boots. When George got sick after hearing about the Wright brothers, Huggins brought him soup and bread and hot coffee every morning before the crew went out for the day. He remembered Huggins saying to him once, "You don't seem the way people told me black fellers would be when I was coming up." And George rolled over under his blanket, wanting to ask Huggins why he thought someone else got to decide the way he was supposed to be, but he did not ask it. "You almost a halfway-decent feller, Hug," he said instead.

After Huggins was thumped stone dead by the big Atlantic white, just the kind of danger he had asked the boy to guard against, George began to spend his leisure hours sitting mournfully at the edge of Lake Drummond. It was not Huggins for whom he mourned, not exactly, for it seemed to him that his mourning was more general; a duller, faded version of the melancholy that had befallen him in the early days of that year. In the evenings he sat and watched the gaslights come on in the fishing shacks that ringed the water's edge. As weak circles of golden light barely brushed back the darkness, he listened to the splash of oars entering water. At sunset he watched the failing light pour through the gaps in the forest that he'd helped make, rays coursing like a spreading flame. He thought he might see the girl in the white canoe, who, as Huggins told it around the fire one evening, paddled effortlessly at the fringes of the lake when the moon was new, searching for her lost love. One afternoon he stumbled on a pair of blue herons tangled in the discarded binding of a timber raft. He took out his elk-antler knife and cut them loose. He watched for a few minutes as their broken wings flailed pathetically and their raspy barks grew to such a fevered desperation that he could stomach them no longer. He turned his back on the crippled birds, on the lake, on the sun setting through the precisely cut gaps in the trees. He thought the knowledge of their agony would overtake all other thoughts and drive him insane, until he felt there was no escape from it but to beat their heads with a cedar branch until they fell soundlessly into the shallow black water.

When he was close to forty years old, and another spring loomed over the swamp, George left the logging camp at Great Dismal for good. Feeling an obligation to Huggins, and already having performed the labor of three lifetimes, he asked the foreman for his pay and if any of Huggins's last effects had been collected that might be returned to his people if any of them could be found. The foreman shrugged and said, "C'mon, George. Don't nobody end up out here in this swamp because we got people waiting on us. We're our only people," he added boldly, but without conviction. "But anyhow," he said, "if a man makes up his mind, I won't be the one to stand in his way. He had some kit we put outside the kitchen, not knowing what to do with it and all."

* * *

The young marine's voice brought George back almost to the present moment, in all its terrible certainty and completeness. The wheels ground and scraped their way around a bend in the rail line. Sparks stippled the darkness, then disappeared outside his window. He did not feel a longing for those days of falling timber in the swamp, but rather a yearning for all the unknown possibilities in his life that fell outside the dominion of memory. What choices might he have made that would have set his life on a different course? A thousand lives he'd never lived passed through his mind and were then immediately gone. Dizzy on the train that rolled through Roanoke Rapids and Rocky Mount, he smelled the brine of a cold Atlantic that conspired with gray sand and skies to almost breach a mostly vacant Provincetown hotel. Him inside of it, this other life, in which he's wiping down a bar of bird's-eye maple while others serve white men, their black hands in white gloves in mahogany smoke-swirled rooms, while one of the white men says to a servant, "All this and I still feel like a fraud."

"...Back in Kansas," Frank was saying, not noticing George's drifting attention, "when I was just a kid, this old fella knows my folks, white guy, he gets me on part-time for Christmas at the post office. Well, I worked the swing shift at the warehouse by the airport, and all day I'd see planes taking off and landing, and nighttime I'd just watch the lights go up and down and listen to those Pratt and Whitneys like they were singing me a lullaby." The marine smiled. He did not tell George that a few years after he fell in love with the DC-3s and Ford Tri-Motors he had watched from the windows of the Topeka Airport's mail warehouse, he would also watch a hundred soldiers from the Chinese People's Volunteer Army run down a hillside, all on fire, screaming like demons from the nightmares of a child, a whole stream of them like tiny burning ants from his perch in the cockpit of his Corsair. They stripped off their quilted napalm-covered uniforms in a wind so cold it seemed to move through the valley as though in a solid state, as though it had transformed into a previously unknown element. He did not tell George, nor would he tell anyone else, not ever, that he had never slept so well as he did that night, having guided his plane through the unassailable darkness to the scratch of dirt they called a runway near Yonpo, his flight suit on the floor of the Quonset hut that was his home in Korea, his body still reeling in the residue of flight.

"Lots changed since I was a young man," said George. "You know, I knew a feller once said he seen the Wright brothers' first flight."

The marine was quiet. He thought of the cold stars above the Chosin Reservoir. "I guess that's progress, sir."

They parted ways in Fayetteville. George got on the evening bus and stepped off two hours later. A yellow moon hung low in the sky. Out of the darkness, the scattered one-story brick buildings that made up Pembroke, North Carolina, appeared. And George went into a diner he had not seen in almost seventy-five years.

THREE

ON THE NIGHT Rawls discovered what had happened to Nurse, a man named Antony Levallois watched a line of lanterns emerge from the woods behind Bob Reid's house. The specks of light floated down the river road that formed the two-mile-long south boundary of Beauvais Plantation. He was tired, but at nearly forty years old had become accustomed to the peculiarities of his life and did not expect them to change. He sometimes attributed his uneasy disposition to loneliness, for though he felt little more than contempt for most of the people he met, he regretted their eventual absence at least as much.

Mr. Levallois went to the stable and knocked on his groom's door. When he heard a shuffle he told the boy to have his horse saddled and brought to the porch. As he leaned against the stone balustrade and rail, it occurred to him that he had not touched another human being in a good long while. Mother and Father were long dead. He had a brother who had returned as a failure to their ancestral home in Nantes nearly twenty years before. He remembered touching a boy and the boy touching him back, in a large wardrobe at the school at number 5 Place du Bouffay where his father sent him to study as a boy, and the letters, seemingly hundreds of them, sent down the Loire and over the Atlantic, that begged his father to let him return to Virginia. He'd bedded a few of his slaves when he was in his twenties to dissipate a foul choleric humor, he told himself; first a beautiful quadroon boy he'd bought on a whim while attending to business near Suffolk, then the boy's mother, then sister, and a few others that made little to no impression on him, for by the time he entered his early thirties he felt his humors had reached a kind of equilibrium and that those base desires were mostly gone. He had never been married. And he had never slept with a white woman.

Even when he considered the way he distributed justice among his slaves, he could not ignore the fact that it was always mediated by some instrument or another: a long pine sapling, a whip, or a pair of shears. Not that this caused him much distress. While he was not a religious man, he did make room for God when he provided the best explanation for a thing that perplexed him. Levallois did not think that his chattels were inherently different from him by constitution, or that they lacked intelligence. He had seen plenty of white men lazier and duller than his best slaves. But he also took it on faith that the state of things was an expression of God's will. What he missed was something he had really never had. He had spent his life making such a production of earning the respect of other men that he now came to resent it if it came slowly, or if it seemed to be obligatory or

performed. He felt with a deep disappointment that whatever he had built was not the same thing as who he was: a
man named Levallois, thirty-nine years old, born near the
intersection of four counties in central Virginia but raised
largely in France, and now getting to a point where the absence of a woman in his life diminished him in the eyes of
other men. He might have thought that this reflected the
ordained state of things as well, but here we have the contradictions of what we might call Mr. Levallois's faith: it was
only strong when it worked clearly in his favor.

He rode his horse across his property to catch up to the
line of lanterns and the riders who carried them. The road
curved off there toward the river on the western end of his
property. After a few minutes of waiting in the road he saw
the gray outlines of four riders emerge through the cold
spring fog, a band of glowing light above the tree line to the
east. He recognized Bob Reid first, and behind him Reid's
neighbor, the tavern keeper Wilson Baker. He knew both
men in passing, Bob Reid perhaps a bit more than that, as
a few acres of his place adjoined Beauvais and he usually
hired him to take his tobacco down to market on the narrow gauge. The other men would have been unlikely to say
the same about Levallois.

The third rider was Pete Rivers, who doubled as both
deputy sheriff and town drunkard. It was common knowledge that Rivers's family had been among the first to settle
this area, back when it had been a refuge for Huguenots the
British wanted to be rid of and a shield between the Indians and Byrd's Virginia planters to the east. Pete could see

a variation of his own name in a graveyard where the old Monacan village once stood, the place where these refugees intended to build a city of their own. Though Rivers's people would survive those first hard years and go on to occupy an important position in the county, he and his father had managed to undo generations of hard work, and Pete now survived on a bitter mixture of the reputation of the dead and the pity of the living. Pete, when drunk, sometimes imagined that city: the permanence of brick, the noon sun a blinding reflection off white sandstone, but it had not been built. His family, like all of the other families that survived, eventually quit the village and burrowed into the solitude of their allotted land. A lonely wall of unblemished forest stretched unending to the west. And after a while they were Americans.

The last rider Levallois saw was Emily. She looked at him briefly, as if he were but one of many features in the land to fall under her appraisal. He was surprised by how competently she controlled her mount, a mottled gray Percheron stallion he thought would have been too large for most men to put under saddle. Though still very much a girl, Emily looked to Levallois like a woman who had once been beautiful. It seemed somehow difficult to see her clearly, as if a thin haze obscured that beauty, rather than the fact that what he really saw in her was more possibility than residue, though each could have diverged from his ideals by a matter of the same degree. The simple geometry of her face meant nothing to him, and neither did her unusual eyes, nor anything about her that he might learn through her companionship. But he felt drawn to her regardless of all that. And though he could not articulate it at that time, perhaps because this attraction was one that would never cross into the territory of thought even up until the day he died, he saw in her both a past and future that could be possessed. To Levallois, she could be anyone he might make her into, but more important she could be everyone. That morning, seeing her on that huge horse on the river road, he pushed against the part of himself that desired Emily Reid, a fourteen-year-old girl, beneath him in every way that could be measured, and detested it. And that is part of what made him who he was. He wanted a blank slate. To possess one girl was a satisfaction received already in a state of decomposition. But to possess them all was something else entirely.

Bob stopped his horse in the road. He took off his hat and offered a good morning to Levallois.

"Trouble, Mr. Reid?" said Levallois.

"My boy seems to have run off. Hope we ain't disturb your sleep," said Reid.

"No, sir. I seldom sleep the night through."

"I had to fetch Mr. Baker and the deputy here to help me hunt for him."

"Damn shame," Levallois said. "World's in a shameful state."

"His momma said he's after some young thing across the county line," said Rivers. "We're headed down to the landing to see if that old Melungeon caught a whiff."

Without invitation Levallois nudged his horse to the

front of the line and spurred it to a brisk trot. The men exchanged curious looks. Wilson Baker shrugged and said, "He's a strange bird, ain't he?" Bob and Pete agreed he was and that was as close as they were willing to get to a comprehensive assessment. They followed him down the road.

Emily hung back a bit as the men rode off. She was excited by their encounter with Mr. Levallois. He was a striking man. Quite tall and dark complected. He wore a neatly trimmed but full mustache. She thought that he might make a good figure for a statue. She had only known of him before through bits of overheard conversation while around adults. *That queer Frenchman,* they'd say. Or, *He's got the whole county all the way up under his boot.* One man might tell another that they had seen him at a distance on a ride, and nothing more. It occurred to Emily that though these were the words they used to talk about him, the one they should have used was echoing through her head, repeated in the same way she'd learned it in her vocabulary lesson with her mother: *deference, deference.* She watched the four riders disappear into the woods as they rode toward the ferry crossing. She spurred her big stallion on, her mind reeling from lack of sleep, for the first time considering that the world might be a game no one knew the rules to, and someone who claimed otherwise was sure to be a liar. Her mind drifted as she rode to catch them. She barely held the reins. The dream came back, partway. A bright sun above the fields. Wings beating the air, terribly.

* * *

Rawls left the old man's cabin on the soybean farm and headed toward the landing not quite two hours before Mr. Levallois encountered Bob's party on the road. He knew he was taking a risk trying to use the bateau ferry as a runaway, but the river was still much too cold to swim across and he did not know where he might find a boat or how to use one if he did. He also knew that the ferryman, the Melungeon named Spanish Jim from up in the mountains, was viewed with a suspicion verging on contempt by most of the white folks he'd heard speak about him. Though this could sometimes cause a man to double down on his disdain for colored folks, it was also occasionally a sign of what passed for compassion in the white man's world.

He stood in the tree line for a while and watched Spanish Jim and a boy lying on their bedrolls next to a sputtering fire. The firelight cast a glow around the meadow where the two figures slept and shimmered where its reflection broke up in the water near the shoreline and the small dock. He stepped out into the meadow, the ferryman's camp about halfway between the woods and the road, and made his way toward where the old man snored noisily. As he stood over the two figures, it occurred to Rawls that he had not considered just exactly what he was going to say to get this man to take him across. He only knew that Nurse was somewhere on the other side. He could get to her. He knew he could, dammit. The dawn-to-dusk pass was still in his shirt pocket. If he could reach the city before another night fell, if he could get to Jackson Ward and slip into the crowd of free black faces, if he could get close enough to the Devil's Half Acre...

"Howdy," a small voice said to him.

Rawls turned and saw the sleeping boy was now sitting upright, looking at him blankly. He did not reply. His body precariously balanced between stillness and potential motion.

"Jim says we run the boat between sunup and sundown." By way of emphasis the boy pointed one small hand upward and the other downward.

"You know if Jim here makes exceptions?" Rawls asked. He reached to the small of his back as if to stretch, feeling the handle of the tobacco knife tucked into his britches. Spanish Jim continued to snore contentedly.

"Ain't studied that word," the boy said, then casually circled the dying fire and nudged at Spanish Jim's side with his bare foot.

The old man grumbled, stretched beneath his blanket, and yawned.

The boy grabbed at his ear and shouted into it, "Wake up, Jim! We got a customer!"

The old man sat up, looked Rawls over, and said, "There's a rooster in them woods yonder. First boat goes across by his say-so."

Rawls looked up the road into the darkness of the woods. "Well, you see, Mr. Jim, I was hoping to get a jump on things this morning…"

Jim put up his hand and stopped him.

It occurred to Rawls that Spanish Jim was the darkest white man he'd ever seen. And it was obvious why some might call him an Indian or a mustee on account of his color, but by studying his features Rawls didn't see how he could be anything but white folks, especially with those blue eyes tucked into all them wrinkles.

The old man held his hand up until all three of them were still and quiet. "Now, young Master Talbot, you listen real good to what I'm about to tell this feller."

"All right, then," said the boy.

Rawls shifted from one foot to the other, readying himself to throw all his weight in either direction and run like hell if the need arose.

Jim went on, saying, "I don't want you to tell me nothing, hear? I damn sure don't want to be making no special trips across this river. The whole course of our conversating ought to go like so, 'Ol' Jim, I'd like to ride that bateau 'cross the river.' And I'll say, 'Well, surely, mister, if you got two bits, I'll clear a space good enough for the Christ Child himself.' You get my meaning?"

"But, you see, I got to be someplace and there might be trouble if I don't get there directly," said Rawls.

Spanish Jim pawed at the scruff on his face. "Listen, friend. I don't want to talk about trouble. There always might be trouble. The good Lord's up there playing dice, far as I can tell. And some kinds of trouble is catching and some ain't. All I'm wanting to hear is that you just a freeman with two bits wanting to cross this river the way a freeman would."

Rawls stopped bouncing between his feet. He forced himself to stand tall and straight and said, "I got two bits and I'd like to cross this here river."

The old man closed his eyes, tilted his brown head toward the impending twilight, and took a deep breath. He smiled, his teeth a checkerboard in his mouth. He walked down to where the boat was tied and fetched a blanket from the boat and brought it back to the fire. "You get up in that tall grass a little ways out from the firelight while I get this old bateau situated," he said to Rawls. "Maybe if some folks come down the road to catch the ferry you might just want to hang back a bit."

"Thank you, sir," Rawls said. He went into the meadow, the grass nearly shoulder height and blowing in the cold breeze away from the fire. He spread out the blanket and looked up at the stars. He thought of Nurse, somewhere in the city, somewhere distant. A feeling which had for most of his conscious life filled up the shape of his mind and heart began to gather and concentrate. He fought sleep, terrified of what he might see if he dreamed of her. At the very center of his being he felt an unimaginable pressure. It seemed to bear down with the weight of all the stars in the sky and reach up from the unknown depths of the earth, beneath the brown bottomland dirt, beneath the stone. He thought he heard his mother's voice. The voice said today would be a hard day, and so would tomorrow.

Spanish Jim and the boy John Talbot untied the ferry from its mooring and made their preparations to push the boat out into the cold brown water. "Did you follow all that, boy?" he asked.

John considered what had transpired as best he could. "That's a free nigger over there wanting us to tote him across?"

"Don't know no different, do we?" said Spanish Jim.

"No, sir, didn't ask."

"We didn't ask 'cause it ain't our business figuring who's free and who ain't. Our business is getting that boat across the river. Understand?"

Less than an hour had passed since Rawls first walked out of the woods toward Spanish Jim and the boy Talbot. The boat was ready. As Spanish Jim turned to whistle for Rawls to come up out of the tall grass, he heard a dog pacing and growling on the road at the edge of the meadow. He stood as still as a pane of glass. "Leave them ropes be, Master Talbot," he told the boy.

John walked toward the dog.

"Don't you walk up on that mutt, Johnny. Can't count on 'em to be predictable." To himself he cursed with a bitterness that would have surprised John if Spanish Jim had allowed him to hear it. Over his long life in Virginia, Spanish Jim had become attuned to the signs of the natural world. He could tell when a squirrel determined he was not a threat by its subtle but predictable sequence of alarm, then silence, then contented chatter. He could smell rain an hour out. And he knew that when a dog on a scent loped out of the morning dark, he was soon to hear the beat of horses' hooves, and then the angry inquisition of the men who rode them. "Come back by me, John," he called out. "I don't want you to get hurt." He took his hat off and crumpled it in a fist by his side. He could not bring himself to look up the road or into the tall grass, so he stared down at one spot on the beaten dirt, waiting.

*   *   *

John Talbot had been told quite often that he was a stupid boy. Perhaps he was, the way he indifferently moved toward the dog as it growled and started to circle at his approach. When the boy had first come to the ferry landing, Spanish Jim thought he might have been feral, raised by bears or a nearby wolf pack. He had heard that kind of thing was possible, and when John strolled up, not much more than six or seven years old, and began picking through Spanish Jim's things, Jim couldn't think of anything to do but beat him off with a stick the way one might do with a raccoon. A few hours passed before John Talbot demonstrated the power of speech. All Jim was able to get out of him were different combinations of the word "dead" and the name Talbot. Over time he began to feel a great deal of responsibility for the boy. He had started by calling him Dumb John out of a kind of habit, even as an expression of affection, an affection that John reliably returned with sincerity and free of complication. Eventually Spanish Jim realized to call him dumb would not work as a corrective, because the child could not comprehend the ways he was deficient, or the profound degree of his deficiency. It would be as useful as telling a blind man that he cannot describe the sky. And anyway, if there was one thing the old man Spanish Jim knew with absolute certainty, it was that the world reminds you of your troubles often enough without even seeming like it tried. So as their lives together fell into a comfortable rhythm he began to call him other names, very often ones he'd heard that people gave to those they loved.

Rawls startled at the sound of Champion's barking. He felt for the tobacco knife, the small, axlike head of it cold between his fingers. Rawls slowly raised his eyes above the waving bluestem. Master Bob and his daughter and three others. Curiously, he chided his master in his mind for involving Emily in this business. Why this one aspect of the scene seemed particularly inappropriate was never resolved for him, because that thought passed very quickly from his mind and was replaced by his wondering whether or not he would die right in that field without ever seeing Nurse again.

The four men slowed their horses at the sight of Talbot, the dog, and Spanish Jim and came up abreast of one another. Emily stopped her horse behind them.

"Morning, gentlemen," the old man greeted them.

"Seems like that boy there's took to your birder, Bob," said Sheriff Rivers. Levallois had pushed the pace, and they'd covered the almost fifteen miles from where they'd met up with him very quickly. Bob smelled liquor on the sheriff's breath and wondered how a man could nip a bottle at the trot they'd been on. Wilson Baker was nervous. The tavern keeper had to put Rivers up after a bender often enough to know how he could get to peacocking behind that badge when he was in his cups. The only reason Wilson Baker was out of his bed that night was as a favor to Bob, on account of the good work Rawls and his mules did with the provisions he hired them to bring down from Richmond.

Levallois dismounted and let his horse graze in the meadow across the road from where Rawls lay trembling in the grass.

"That dog just strolled up like it was nobody's business. I guess the boy took it for a stray," said Jim.

"What's your name, youngster?" asked Wilson Baker.

"Gentlemen, allow me to present my apprentice, John Talbot," replied Jim.

Levallois unsaddled his horse, put the saddle in the dirt at the edge of the road, and sat on it comfortably. He lit a pipe and puffed hard a few times to get it going. Spanish Jim smiled nervously. It seemed odd to him, the man sitting there while the others remained on horseback, as if the search for Bob's runaway was an afterthought to him, or he had become bored by the whole endeavor. Jim knew all these men by sight, and though none of them but Sheriff Rivers had ever given him trouble, he was especially wary of this man Levallois. Spanish Jim had lived for many years as a man whose complexion did not grant him the benefit of the doubt. He did not know if his people were truly Portuguese or East Indians or the last remnants of a lost tribe of Israel, but he had allowed those things to be said often enough when he was a young man in the backcountry of Virginia that he was begrudgingly accorded many of the rights of a white man, and those he was not were simply a reminder that he must always be on guard against the curiosity his appearance inspired in others, for the behavior it inspired might be the biggest curiosity of all. The only roofs he'd slept beneath since he'd left his family farm up by the Cowpasture River in Botetourt County, as a fifteen-year-old, had been those erected above jail cells. And he'd stood before enough magistrates to learn the difference between the kind of men who wanted only to collect power and the far-more-dangerous ones who wanted only to collect the wants of other men.

"You speak, son?" Bob asked Talbot.

John Talbot did not respond but looked to Spanish Jim for some clue as to the source of all this commotion. Champion had settled at his feet and gone to sleep. Emily looked at her dog and the dim-witted boy just a few years older than herself. John caught her eye on him and was transfixed.

"Sheriff," asked Levallois from his saddle on the ground, "might I inquire something of old Spanish Jim?"

Sheriff Rivers's agitation calmed. "By all means, Mr. Levallois, but I ain't heard straight talk from no damn Melungeon in my life."

"How are your eyes?" Levallois asked Spanish Jim.

"They do what I need 'em to, I suppose."

"So would it be fair to say that your eyes took in the collar on that dog?"

"I guess they did."

"Then are you ignorant of the signifiers of ownership?"

Rawls felt the pressure return. It seemed to move out of his body and expand into an orbit around him, the old man and the boy, the horses and their riders, until it enclosed what he knew of the world surrounding them. He thought that if he did not come out right then they would kill Spanish Jim, and maybe the boy, too, but the pressure spinning around the whole world still held him down to the brown dirt he had unconsciously clutched two fistfuls of.

"Didn't see no owner till now. Ain't claimed no ownership of man or beast in my life," said Jim.

"What about your young apprentice?"

"He can scoot off any time he likes."

The boy, as he often did, misunderstood, thinking perhaps Spanish Jim was saying he no longer desired his company.

"And of course your people would have made it clear that a white boy like this can't be owned," said Levallois.

"My people all been dead since I was a pup about his age. Burned out of our cabin on Floyd Mountain sometime before this last century come in."

"And what if a black boy, maybe teenage, came down this road. Would you know what signified ownership then?"

"I been in this world a long time, but never once have I seen a dog collar on a black boy yet."

"You might watch yourself, Jim," said Reid. "We're looking for my boy and that's it. Don't get yourself mixed up in it with that sass."

Levallois stood up and knocked the remaining tobacco from his pipe.

Emily caught a sniff of it in the air and thought it smelled very sweet. She was half asleep in her saddle, but the whole affair seemed to her a great adventure. She looked over at her father. He seemed timid and uncertain. Perhaps because there are no mules around to whip, she thought. His hand nervously palmed the stock of his shotgun in its scabbard, which annoyed her. She had the sense that whatever Mr. Levallois wanted to happen would happen. What was there to be so nervous about?

Levallois walked over to Spanish Jim and said to him out of the earshot of the others gathered at the ferry landing, "You're going to want to call for him to come up out of that grass or it's going to happen again."

Spanish Jim wanted to ask what would happen again, but he was too busy looking at the blood on the blade of the small knife Levallois was wiping with his handkerchief. It looked to Jim to be a very expensive knife, delicate even, with a handle made from an elk's antler and a blade so fine he had not even felt it enter the space between his ribs on the left side of his body. Jim fell to his knees. *I didn't ask his name,* he tried to say, but it sounded to him instead like wind whistling over the water where the Cowpasture and Jackson Rivers met to make the James.

"Anything you'd like to contribute, Jim?" Levallois asked. The strike had been so quick that the others had not seen it. He stabbed him again.

"What in the hell are you doing!" said Bob. "Look away, Emily. Look away!" he shouted. He pulled his shotgun halfway out, but Wilson gave him a nervous look and said, "Easy, Bob. Go easy." He let it slide back in the scabbard, saying, "Look, Mr. Levallois, I just want to find Rawls and carry him back to my place."

"I'm just trying to give you the help you asked for, Mr.

Reid, in a neighborly way." If anyone recalled that they had not asked for his help, it was not mentioned. Levallois seemed to vibrate, and the earth seemed to shake along with him, though it was only the exhaustion that had begun to warp the perceptions of those gathered at the ferry landing. Rawls felt the vibration, though. He listened to the terrible sound of Spanish Jim's blood falling drop by drop into the scales of justice that would weigh his fate. He thought of Nurse in the whipping room at Lumpkin's Jail. And he heard his mother saying that it would be a hard day today, and a hard one tomorrow, too. All his life had been a punishment, and though he had often told himself that what was meant for him could fall on anyone at any time, thus far his allotment of cruelty and injustice had not been given to anyone else. But now the old man lay bleeding in the road. Spanish Jim had done Rawls no harm. He was simply going to take him to the other side of the river for the same two bits as anyone else. Rawls did not know what people deserved, but he knew they did not get it. Instead they seemed to get what they did not deserve, as if the world had been built that way like a machine that could produce only one outcome. He hoped that he might see Nurse again in the hereafter, but he did not think it would be so. He stood up and walked out of the tall grass and onto the road. Champion did not move toward him. She stayed with John Talbot who was now kneeling and sobbing over a prostrate Spanish Jim and the pool of his blood collecting in the dust of the road. He looked at Bob, who had paid three hundred fifty dollars to own him, and said, "Do whatever you got to do, Master Bob, but do it quickly."

Bob and Wilson Baker tied Rawls's hands and feet and slung him sideways over Emily's horse. They left John Talbot with Spanish Jim. "We'll get a doctor down here, son," said Bob. Champion stayed by John Talbot's side.

They left a cloud of dust behind that settled slowly onto the nearby blades of grass and down onto the wet blood in the road. It fell into John's hair and he blinked his eyes against it. He watched the riders until they disappeared around a bend in the road and then looked down at Spanish Jim.

"I believe it's gonna be a warm one, Jim," said Talbot. And Jim said, "I believe you might be right, Master Talbot," by which he meant, of course, that he felt that knowing the boy had been the best thing that had ever happened in his life; Spanish Jim, the Melungeon from Botetourt County who'd been burned out of his home in 1800 by men who spit on his dead father's body and laughed as they said, "Here lies Emmett Collins, King Turd of Shit Mountain." That was what he thought, what a good child this dimwit John had been to him, he who had never known a roof of his own in his life, and never owned either man nor beast nor anything except the bateau boat he used to ferry folks across the James.

Emily rode back to her father's house with Mr. Levallois, who smelled sweetly of tobacco. She felt sorry for the Talbot boy, but she was sure the old man must have done something terrible.

*　　*　　*

They made it back to Bob Reid's place late in the morning. Levallois introduced himself to Mrs. Reid with a show of formality. "I regret we have not met before now," he said. "Your husband does good work when I need it. Good work indeed." To Bob he said, "And here you have been hiding a great beauty from me this whole time!" Lucy Reid blushed and took Emily into the house. He watched the front door for a few moments after it closed, then turned back and took a seat on the porch steps. He crossed his left leg over his right, casually, and packed another pipe.

Wilson Baker pulled Rawls down from the horse and propped him up against the tree Champion spent most of her nights chained to.

"Let him be from that rope there, Mr. Baker," said Levallois.

None of the other three knew what to do next. They had all lived a long time under the assumption that the threat of retribution was enough of a deterrent to keep the course of their lives moving in a predictable direction. And further, that their hesitance to use violence to enforce their mastery over those they owned was a sign of a deep well of kindness and loyalty that characterized the tangled knot of the relationships of all involved. Among the five men gathered beneath the colorless buds of the sycamore tree, only two were free of this delusion.

Rawls sat covered in dirt and sweat. The spring air blew cold through the tatters of his shirt. It was precisely Mr.

Reid's equivocation that made him want to run again at night. He would admit that he did not know much about the world, but he had decided long before that a kind master was a terrible master to have. And Bob Reid was worse than that. He had fooled himself into thinking he was not really a master at all. The butcher who had taken the hatchet to his feet as a boy had demanded obedience. Kind masters, he had heard, demand devotion. But Master Reid seemed to think he'd earned Rawls's consent. As if the pieces of paper in Bob's safe with his name on it (and the ones with his mother's, too) were merely a formality. How sometimes, as they rode on the mule cart toward the city, he'd say, "You know, Rawls, if John Brown had got his way, I'd still want to have you working for me anyway, even as a paid man." Rawls hated this notion more than anything; that if white folks just believed they would be good in a different world, a world that did not exist, then that made them good in the one that did. He muttered to himself, "Get on with it, then, you devils, if you got the starch for it."

Levallois slapped his knee and got stuck between laughing and choking on his pipe smoke. It poured out of his mouth and nostrils. "Hear that, Bob?" he said. "Doesn't that just beat all hollow?"

Rawls stiffened as Levallois rose from the porch steps.

"You can't beat the pride out of a boy like this. It would be a sin. Think of what he could do when properly motivated." He was talking to Bob, but it was not lost on Rawls that he was Levallois's true intended audience. "I think we've gotten into a bad habit. And when I say 'we' I mean all of us southern men, myself included. We might turn course right here and now. Set things straight for a hundred years more." He was pacing now, leaning into every word as if it came to him through a revelation. "The Yanks look down on us from amongst their tangle of machinery, thinking we treat the whole world like a barnyard, thinking we don't know a thing about enterprise and progress. And maybe they've been right. Don't you remember that Gabriel nigger plotting murder in Henrico? It wasn't so long ago. And Nat Turner chopping up white women and babies down in Southampton?"

"Come on now, Mr. Levallois," Sheriff Rivers interrupted, "we can't have rebellion without something being done about it."

"Too true, Pete," Levallois said. "When I was ten years old I saw a piece of Turner hanging from a lamppost. Could have been a pork shoulder, way it was up there swinging. What I mean is that the Yanks don't destroy a machine that malfunctions if it can be repaired, do they? Well, I'll tell you, I've been to New York City, and I've never seen them chop up a cotton gin and hang bits of it from a lamppost." He walked over to Rawls, grabbed him by the shoulders, and stood him up. Rawls did not falter. Levallois whispered in his ear, "How much starch you think I got, boy?"

"Plenty. I know what you are," said Rawls.

"Good," he said. Levallois turned to Bob and said, "I think this boy can be fixed. But we've got to figure out the source of his malfunction."

"That'd be a start, I guess," said Bob.

"Who taught you your manners, Bob?"

"My manners?"

"Yes, Bob. Your place, your way of being in the world. How about you, Sheriff? Mr. Baker?"

"I'd say my momma," said Wilson Baker.

Rawls sat back down without asking permission. A breeze still blew through the clearing, cold and constant. He caught the sheriff's scent. Bad breath and liquor sweat. The stink of soiled clothes. He felt the air touch every pore on his body. He knew what was coming. Thoughts of Nurse filled his head. His mother saying it would be a hard day today, and a hard one tomorrow. It was always going to end this way. An appointment was being kept that he had not known about, but it was being kept. His breath caught in his chest. His heart fluttered like a shot dove. Am I who I thought I was, or will I cower like the rest?

"That's what I would have said, Mr. Baker. Your mother made you the way you are. The way a machine might make an object useful to the world?"

"I never thought of it like that, but I suppose that's true."

"And if a machine is making defective objects, we might just say the damage could be irreparable."

"I suppose we might."

"Young Rawls here, he's not an old machine. He's got steam in his boiler for days. But his momma? Maybe there's something wrong with her if he keeps acting like this. Maybe she just can't raise a child up. And Bob, you got her tending to young Emily there. Rawls, you think your master's going to let your momma tend to his daughter when she's liable to malfunction? I think we ought to take her apart and see if we can figure the problem. One little bit at a time. Yes, sir, when an old machine breaks down you have got to take it apart. You might not get it back together properly, but you've got to try. Unless we're wrong about her. Unless you mean to tell me she raised her child right."

Rawls began to cry noiselessly. He felt a rage unlike any he had ever felt. He figured he could get his hands on one, tied up or not. The sheriff. Maybe choke the life out of him before the others killed him. What was the point of all this? Each breath. Each bruise and cut. Each irreparable wound to his heart. His momma would understand if he went for one, he thought. If I see her in the by-and-by, she'd understand.

None of the other men resisted Levallois's escalation, not even the sheriff, who was as malleable in the face of real authority as a dog trained on beef liver.

"Or maybe there's another way," said Levallois. The world is changing, he thought. And though he was willing to admit it more quickly than most, his real gift was in recognizing that people were not changing with it. Stone gave way to bronze. The wagon gives way to the railway car. But people are forever fixed in their desires. One way or another, we will all have to pay for what we want. "Bob," he said, and then paused as if to indicate the intensity of his concentration, "I'll give you double what you paid for the pair."

Later that day Levallois paid Bob Reid a little less than fourteen hundred dollars for the papers on Rawls, Aurelia, and the big Percheron Emily had ridden with them in the night. That sum was a thousand dollars more than Aurelia's price, then pregnant with Rawls, when she was bought from Lumpkin's almost twenty years before. When they arrived at Beauvais that evening, Levallois told Rawls what was expected of him and what he could expect in return. "I'm a businessman, after all, Rawls," he said. "And life is a series of bargains." This was a few weeks before April of 1861. War was coming. Levallois counted back the years in his mind, figuring out the interest and appreciation on his new assets. He was pleased. Accounting for inflation, he damn near got the horse for free.

FOUR

GEORGE STOOD IN a gravel parking lot in front of a diner waiting for the hostess to finish the fifth Pall Mall she'd smoked in the ten minutes before 6:00 a.m. arrived. She looked at her watch, tossed her smoke on the asphalt, rubbed it out with the toe of her baby-doll pump, and gave him a nod to follow her inside. The cooks had come in the back way, he guessed, and they oiled up and scraped the flattop, cracked a few eggs, and settled into their prep work. Two waitresses followed after them, one of whom was the girl's mother, George would discover later, and they sat down at the counter rolling silverware in napkins.

The girl with the Pall Malls sized him up for a minute, reached some kind of decision, and led him to a booth in the back. They passed a sign on their way to the table that read CROATAN. George looked around the restaurant when he sat down and saw another sign that read COLORED more or less on the other side of the diner from where he'd been seated by the girl. He saw no sign for whites. "What's with the signs?" he asked the girl.

"Law says we got to have separate sections for white folks, Indians, and black folks," she said.

"Where's the white section?"

"Well, it's mostly Croatan around these parts. Black folks, too. But white folks?" She laughed. "They don't come in here." He might as well have asked where the pope of Rome sat.

She walked over to a chromed-out Seabird jukebox in the corner. Her black hair fell over her shoulders and covered the record case. She dropped in three nickels, punched the keys, and three very fine country-and-western songs filled up the nearly empty diner. The oldest waitress brought him coffee. She had her gray hair tied in a long plait with a piece of ribbon. George asked her about the song that had just started playing. He couldn't identify one of the instruments. She told him it was Webb Pierce singing "Slowly," that the strange bending notes were made on a newfangled guitar called a pedal steel, and that she had developed this expert knowledge because the hostess, her daughter Lottie, had played it incessantly every time she'd had a shift since March. George was not much for Victrolas or radios. He didn't dislike them, but throughout most of his time on earth music was a temporary interruption, an aspect of life in which choice remained a factor. Over the last twenty or thirty years he sometimes felt as though he'd entered into a new category of wilderness, in that the world continued to indifferently add to the list of things he could not control, until even a private thought had to fight for space against the noise and neon. For his seventieth birthday his wife had surprised him with a Lincoln-Zephyr sedan that came with a Motorola radio, and their last argument before she died had been about him slapping her hand away from the dial because he would not let her turn it on.

George pulled out *The Negro Travelers' Green Book* from his small suitcase and set it on the Formica table under the window next to the salt and pepper shakers. He then took out the other book he'd brought with him. It was a copy of the diary of William Byrd II of Westover, which George found useful mostly for the way its weight functioned as a preservative for his oldest possession, the aforementioned note requesting that whoever might find the boy he had once been look after him. It was a fragile thing, the note, both as a physical object barely resisting the corrosive effect of time and in the desperation implicit in the fact of its having been written at all. With a shaking hand someone had scrawled out the following: *1866. My name is George. I'm nearly three years old. Look after me. I now belong to you.* Unlike the book itself, George hoped to put the note to use, though he remained unsure of how he might do so.

Henry Levy the second, who he had been quite friendly with, had given the book to him in the forties, after mistaking George's ceaseless curiosity about his own past for a wider interest in the history of Virginia, and especially that concerning the linkage between it and North Carolina. George had thanked him very kindly for the gift, appreciating his friend's gesture very much, but he had a deeply ingrained skepticism toward history, given that very little of it that he encountered reflected the singular experience of passing through it. He much preferred the adventures of Dumas, though he was far too much a gentleman to say so to Henry.

Lottie moved to a seat at the end of the counter close to George. Her mother brought out a plate and set it next to the book. George ate slowly. He stared out the big plate windows into the sunny morning. His desire to recall his draw to the place was matched by his inability to do so. How do you begin to search for something lost when you don't know what it is that's missing? He now found himself in a roadside diner, another forlorn country song playing thinly in the air, uncertain of what, exactly, he was supposed to do next.

"What's that book?" asked Lottie.

"Nothing much," George said.

"That's a lot of book for nothing much," she said, snubbing out her cigarette.

"That's why it's useful. Holds this note down so I don't lose it."

"What's the note, then, if you don't mind me asking?" She hopped down off the stool and slid into the bench opposite George.

"Old-man stuff, I guess," he said. He passed it over to her.

She held it carefully. "Who's George?" she asked.

"That'd be me."

She looked incredulous. "Eighteen sixty-six? Can't be. Can it?"

"You never met an old man before?"

"Well, sure I have. It's just that, and I don't mean to be

rude, mister, but 1866 might as well be feudal England, it seems so long ago."

George laughed. "You ain't wrong about how long ago it seems."

"So that'd make you, what, ninety-two or ninety-three years old?"

"Thereabouts."

"Well, when's your birthday?"

"I don't rightly know. That note you're holding is all I know about where I come from, excepting I somehow ended up around these parts as a boy."

"You don't recall your people?" Lottie asked.

Those moments he was able to recall from his life were fleeting and episodic. They seemed unconnected, as if they had happened to someone else, though he sometimes imagined that by looking back he could impose some order on them. Know thyself, he'd heard a million times. Yes. Good luck with that.

The diary of William Byrd II of Westover still sat open on the table between them, though they never acknowledged it, and it is doubtful either of them bothered to read the passage it lay open to, which was as follows:

November 13, 1710. I rose at 7 o'clock and said a short prayer. Then I took a little walk about the plantation. Colonel Digges sent for a white negro for us to see who except the color was featured like other negroes. She told us that in her country, which is called Aboh near Calabar, there were many whites as well as blacks.

*Yesterday Mr. Ingles had a child burnt to death. We
went to the capitol and stayed there about two hours
and then I went and dined with the Governor where I
ate roast mutton. I had a letter from home which told
me all was well except a negro woman who ran away
and was found dead. I said my prayers and had good
health, good thoughts, and good humor, thank God
Almighty.*

He did remember voices in the woods, a noise like rolls
of thunder coming sharply and in quick succession. There
were cries of pain, too, and a man who only called him
"friend" tucking him papooselike into a great gray overcoat
against the cold. The whole world smelled like burned pow-
der, a scent that would subsequently send him reeling into
the past toward that obscure moment for the rest of his life,
and he would have thought that the noise had somehow
strangely struck him blind, were it not for the music of the
horses' hooves that led them into thin blue winter light and
gave him back his vision, where he saw that he was among
six riders emerging from a pall of morning fog and smoking
guns, headed toward a world that seemed unfit for human
habitation.

They passed no cities and no towns. The southern coastal
plains were deep in the bleakness of midwinter. The harvest
had long since come and gone on all the farms. Stubs of
corn and bare dirt were all that remained to break up the

ocean of loblolly and longleaf pines through which they rode, noiseless now, without speech or celebration, and the glide of the horses' hooves through the fallen needles sent the young George into a deep, untroubled sleep.

When he woke he peered out of a gap between two of the many dull brass buttons on the man's wool coat. Had he been old enough to know his letters, he might have seen that the buttons were embossed with csa, though it is unlikely that such knowledge would have meant that much to him. George was cradled inside the coat, the man's left arm supporting his back with his right hand on the reins. He rode tall in the saddle, proudly even, and did not seem bothered at all by the dark red stain on his shoulder that spread ever so slightly with each passing minute. A long time spent in this quiet. Day became night and the air grew colder. The man never looked at George, though from time to time he made a little hup sound and would lift him up a bit so as to make him more comfortable in his curious travel arrangements.

To the child in his coat, it might have seemed as though they had ridden for a thousand years, but Edgar Seldom figured they'd made it more like fifty miles in the fifteen hours since they shot it out with a band of unreformed Confederates roaming the countryside around Great Dismal above the border in Virginia. Edgar shivered at the cold, and at the scene from which they'd plucked the terrified child the day before. The vision of the strange young man, the blood-spattered glasses that he wore, persisted in his mind. How they had found the whole band dancing and whooping over those poor souls. The savagery done to the bodies. When the young man turned a pistol toward him, he had said, "What kind of look is that you giving me, mister?"

"War's been over damn near a year, now," Edgar replied. "You got no cause to do these folks like this."

The young man had laughed then, and Edgar nearly lost himself in the black void of the pistol's barrel, like a traveler searching for Polaris on a night without stars. But Edgar was alive still, despite his wound, and that little bastard wasn't.

He whistled once, and the group of riders slowed, then stopped. That night they set up camp to ride out the rest of winter in the deep woods outside of Edenton. Years had passed since they had been in one spot for more than a week. But it was a new year and they now had a three-year-old boy to watch over, according to the note pinned to his britches when they'd found him. They lit no fire and made no sound at first. The warm blanket into which young George was wrapped and tucked away for sleep that night had been removed from beneath his Confederate colonel's saddle by Edgar at a place in Virginia called Cedar Mountain a few years earlier. As his cousin Charlie wrapped the wound left in his shoulder by the .36 Navy Colt he'd been shot with the day before, Edgar pondered the ways in which this little one's presence might alter their admittedly haphazard undertaking. He, of course, knew by now that there was a price on each of their heads, and that his head, apparently, had the highest value; they'd seen the wanted posters, and had read the earnest editorials calling for the end, by any means, of what was by then being referred to as "the

Seldom Brothers' Rebellion," "the Croatan Rampage," or "Edgar's Revenge."

It seemed to Edgar that they were bound to hang. Though he was in no hurry for that day to come, whenever he reached into his pocket and reread the letter he'd received from his young wife before the fight at Cedar Mountain, he could feel no reason for delay. A line here or a line there, reading *We think we could not suffer more and then we do, they have herded all our hogs onto their land and called us thieves, torches circle the house at night. Dearest Edgar, fear has become the chief attribute of our lives.*

He'd shown the letter to his colonel, and after some platitudes on sacrifice the man said that Edgar was needed for the greater good, and that if he released every man missed by his family there would be no one left to fight the Yankees. Edgar replied that he didn't much care about the Yankees, since they weren't the ones causing trouble for his wife. The officer said, "I would advise you against doing anything rash."

When the fight started the next day, he shot the horse out from under his colonel, took the man's saddle blanket and pair of LeMat pistols while he was still trapped under the dying horse, and walked down the mountain to begin his journey home. A month later he arrived at the house of ash that had replaced his own along the Lumber River in Robeson County. The fields burned. The hogpen posts ripped up out of the ground and used to make the fire in the house burn hotter. No one would say where his wife had gone, or if she'd made it out at all. Most of his kin settled in a wide orbit around his grief, the way one gives a shot buck time to either get up again or die. The last thing anyone wanted to do was walk up on him while he was making up his mind, knowing as they did that there's no better way than that to get the antlers. Only his young brothers, barely teenage, and two cousins were bold enough to speak to him through the trembling silence he pushed out toward the world.

They said the conscription officers had been causing hell for everyone. You couldn't help nobody with nothing or they'd lock you up for associating and ship you off to hard labor in Wilmington. "Shit, Edgar," his cousin Charlie said, "they running through so many goddamn crackers on the line they ain't got none left to do the work. They've rounded up the black folks already. Don't matter if you're free or not. And they ain't even paying the masters when they take them out the fields. They started taking Croatan folks a few months back. Your brother said they went through the Indian school outside Lumberton rounding up boys younger than him. Next day they were looking for the rest of us and set upon your house." And here Edgar was a deserter to boot. If they were rounding up Croatan Indians, Edgar figured he was bound for special treatment and began to think of an appropriate response.

He camped in the clearing next to the wreckage of his house. By day he sifted through the ash. By night he bathed in the river, and the soot came off him in blooms so wide and deep they dulled the moon as it reflected off the already dark water. Before the law came down again on the ruins of his house that warm September day in '62,

Edgar found a slim, fire-bleached finger bone in the ashes and took it down to the river. He did not know what to do or if there was any way to douse the fire the discovery of the bone had stoked inside his chest. He leaned against a tree along the water's edge and sat there till the sun went down, until the lightning bugs arranged themselves like a minor constellation. They hovered over the murky water and pulsed and flashed as if by magic. He decided, deliberately and without regret, to make those responsible feel an amount of pain that would exactly equal in proportion the love he had felt for his wife. Soon enough he would see that there was no way to quantify the infinite and formless pulse that had filled him from the day he first saw her, a young girl bathing in a gingham dress in the Lumber River, the heat having taken physical form in a haze around her face and hair, which was dark and wet with amber water. And what they took from him could not be counted either, but he vowed to make an effort at the calculations anyway. They came around again a week later. The boys would be shipped off to dig trenches or labor on the docks. And Edgar to the gallows. Ten Seldom boys were there that day. Eight left Edgar's camp when the shooting stopped. After all that had transpired in the almost four years since, the remaining six woke from a fitful rest in the woods just west of Edenton to watch the sun come up over the Albemarle Sound.

George poked his fingers through the holes in the striped blanket. He looked over at the man who had carried him the night before. His hair was black and stringy and had no shine. He was filthy just about everywhere visible, as were the others.

George asked something in a timid voice, barely out of babble.

Edgar was startled. No one had spoken for almost twenty-four hours. He only heard the word "home" clearly. "Where's home, friend?" he asked.

The boy did not reply, but instead shrugged and toddled over and sat at Edgar's leg, where Edgar fed him from his own bowl.

"I don't know either," Edgar said. "We're just gonna have to find you one."

The Seldom Gang left the winter camp they'd made along the Albemarle Sound as spring returned. They rode slowly south on thin strips of land above the marshes, sometimes close enough to open water that they could see the barrier islands in the distance. "They got ponies on them islands," Edgar said to George one day, hoping to cheer the boy from the doldrums that seemed to make up the greater part of his disposition. It did not work. George instead imagined horses exiled from the land, their heads struggling through the low chop of gray water in the bay, cursed to swim ever farther out to sea.

Thompson Seldom rode up next to his brother and pinched the boy on his cheeks. George adopted Edgar's posture, but in miniature, sitting upright and holding on to the pommel as they rode, then slouching back into the folds of Edgar's coat. "We got to do something with the feller, Ed. He already made it out of one scrape. He's been all right holed up here with us, but with the whole world after us it'd be a sin to put him in the middle of what we got coming," said Thompson.

"I know it, Brother. But it ain't like we can just set the feller by the side of the road. Only place I know to take him is back to Lumberton."

Thompson scoffed. "Dammit, Ed. We gonna get shot to shit if we go back there."

"You want to take him back to Virginia?" asked Edgar. "Look at him, Tommy. Where else in the world is this boy gonna get treated right? For two hundred years Croatan and black folks been living free in Robeson County, North Carolina. War's been over since last April. If we can get him there without all hell coming down on us, he ought to be left alone. I'm tired of hiding, Brother. And besides, last I checked we were carrying guns, too."

"Edgar," Thompson said, "just don't forget that we ain't all as eager to get to where we're going as you."

They all eventually agreed. And though what was coming for them would find them in the mountains a few months later, they were gifted with a respite from all that for a little while, and they lived the last allotment of their time on earth fearlessly, in the realm of the possible, refusing to look over their shoulders as they slowly made their way home.

They crossed the border into Robeson County in May. Thompson and Charlie both asked Edgar if they ought not keep to the woods, but Edgar felt that if they were going to ask the boy to let this place be his home, they should treat it like a place one need not be afraid of. He did make one concession, though, passing little George to Thompson and telling him to keep back a ways so they could make a break for it if there was trouble.

Edgar guided the procession down the dusty road that led to town. It was oppressively hot, unseasonably so for May, and at first no one seemed the least bit interested in the presence of the riders. They had been on the run since well before the war ended, and though a large plurality of the people in that part of North Carolina had never been truly invested in the cause, it seemed that the effects of the defeat were indiscriminately contagious.

Still, a group of men carefully watched them pass from the wood-plank walkway out front of Greene's Provision and Supply. As the riders neared, Edgar heard a voice call out, "Is that you, Edgar Seldom?" The voice belonged to Mr. Greene, the proprietor and a man long known by Edgar and his people.

"Best I can tell," he replied.

"Y'all back for good?"

Edgar reached down to the scabbard beneath his right leg and quite conspicuously toyed with the stock of his side-by-side. He then halted his horse and rubbed his right hand through his long dark hair, which fell nearly level with the end of his full beard. The gesture exposed the two LeMat pistols he kept tucked into his belt. "Not just now, Mr. Greene. I don't think so anyway," he said.

"People too wore out for trouble, Ed," said Mr. Greene, though Edgar was not sure if that statement was meant to reassure him he'd be free from harm, or if it was an indirect way of Mr. Greene asking not to be included in his retribution.

"Count me in that number," said Edgar.

"Most of them folks who gave you all that guff are dead..."

"Shameful," another man said.

"Indeed. Sinners all," Mr. Greene continued. "And the ones who lived, well, they went looking for wool and come back shorn."

"Guff, you say?" Edgar's heart thrashed around inside his chest like a fox caught in a foot trap. His arms broke out in goose pimples despite the heat. "You know, I think I heard something about those fellers getting killed," Edgar said. "Heard getting killed was catching for a good long while there."

Two of the men on the boardwalk slowly put a little distance between themselves and Mr. Greene. "You go on and ask anyone, Edgar," Mr. Greene said. "No one's causing trouble for any Croatan folks. Hell, we're even letting the niggers be, even though they dragged us into that damn war."

Edgar laughed. "Well, I'm sure we all appreciate it very kindly," he said, and spurred on his horse.

After the cloud of dust subsided, and the riders were clear of town, the men gathered in front of Greene's Provision and Supply simultaneously exhaled the collective breath they'd been holding. "Goddamn," one of them exclaimed, "I thought it was about to jump off for sure."

"I ain't waiting to give him another go," said Mr. Greene, who then trotted across the road to the bank where the small telegraph office had a clerk.

Edgar and his kin rode out toward the river under the light-shot curtains of moss that hung from the live oaks and cypresses. Edgar figured they had a whole day, maybe two if they were lucky.

"So what's the plan, Brother?" Thompson asked.

"You remember Miss Dolores?"

"Sure. She used to scare the ever-living shit out of me. Thought she was mixed up in all kinds of hoodoo."

"Naw," said Edgar. "She's just lived a long time alone."

"What's she got to do with us?" asked Thompson.

"Nothing. That's the point. And I'm hoping she might want some company."

Thompson grabbed the boy up under his arms and tossed him in the air above his saddle, catching him and repeating the process until George laughed uncontrollably. He put his hand on the little boy's shoulder and settled him back into his perch just behind the pommel, gave it a firm but gentle squeeze, and said to no one in particular, "I hope you have a good life, George."

It took them nearly an hour on the poorly tended roads through the swamps around the Lumber River to reach Miss Dolores's cabin. They roped their horses a little ways back from the house, and Edgar approached the stairs that led up to her porch alone.

He called her name and she came to the door. She was of an indeterminate age, and depending on the angle at which she stood, it was also impossible to say whether she was Croatan, mustee, white folks, or some other variety of person Edgar would not know what to call. This bothered people, and for a long time she had withdrawn from the world and its curious but predictable frustration with uncertainty.

"Do you know me, ma'am?" asked Edgar.

"I do," she said.

"I've come to ask you for a favor."

"Do I owe you one?" she asked.

"No. I've been about settling my accounts and I'm sure you owe me nothing."

"I heard about your trouble."

"Yes," he said.

"Your wife was a pretty thing. A good, God-fearing girl."

"She was."

"She ain't come back, has she?"

"No, ma'am. Home Guard killed her when I was up in Virginia back in the war."

"Ah. I see," the woman said. "What's that favor, then?"

"We got a foundling here."

Thompson set the boy down and whispered in his ear. George ran across a few yards of open ground to Edgar and wrapped himself around his leg, where he spun on it as though it were a maypole. The boy looked curiously at the woman.

"So you know where you're heading, then?"

"We do."

"How long you think?"

"We need to be gone soon. After that...I don't know. It's coming one way or another."

"It never works. But you know that now, I suspect?"

Edgar hung his head. And though "shame" is the closest word we have for what he felt, it was not exactly that. "I do," he answered her.

She came down the steps and picked up the boy and held him tightly. "What's his name?" she asked.

"His name is George," he said. A moment later he added, almost as an afterthought, "It's George Seldom." Edgar handed the woman the note they'd found pinned to the small boy's clothes when they'd discovered him hiding under his dead mother's skirts. He had been covered in her blood, awash in it, instinctively holding a small knife with a handle of elk antler. The blade had blood on it, though it was long dried by the time they pulled George from beneath that poor woman's skirts. Blood stained the note as well. Edgar had insisted they stop to wash the child off, so they bathed him in some unnamed icy creek that straddled the dividing line between North Carolina and Virginia. The boy screamed until his tiny voice went hoarse. They wrapped the child in as many warm clothes as they could spare. They were all a little colder that January, but they didn't mind as much as they might have. He asked Miss Dolores to hold the knife for the child until he was older. "It's a fine knife. He ought to have a fine thing like that," he said.

Edgar put his hands on the child's cheeks and looked at Miss Dolores in lieu of thanks. She reached up with her free hand and held his own cheek as if Edgar were a small child again himself. He dropped his head to his chest, and his shoulders slumped inward. His brothers saw Edgar racked and silent from where they stood with the horses, and they supposed that they were watching whatever fire that remained in him go out.

"One good thing still counts," she said. "Now go."

And so they did, their toes dipped already into the water of what awaits us all.

In a photograph taken six months later, and subsequently printed widely in newspapers of the day, Edgar Seldom, his two younger brothers, and his cousin Charles Bride were seen arranged in a row of hastily built, plain pine coffins standing upright against the unpainted wooden walls that housed the Buncombe County Sheriff's Office in the town of Asheville. The eldest, Edgar, was twenty-two years old. The youngest, his brother Thompson Septimus Seldom, was fifteen. Each man had a noose fashioned around his neck, and the distress caused by their bodies being hung and left to swing for three days from a copse of tulip poplars on the east bank of the French Broad River was plain for all to see. Conspicuous, too, were the numerous bullet holes in their bloodstained shirts, about their faces and heads, and, in the case of young Thompson, in his hands and forearms, which in the photograph were exposed below the short sleeves of his undershirt, each of the men having been killed by the deputized posse that found them bathing unarmed in the river just below the copse of trees from which the corpses were then immediately hung. Further reports and editorials suggested that the grotesque nature of the picture was offensive to the sensibilities of the educated readership of several papers internationally, and that, while certainly a righteous blow had been struck for justice, it might have been more prudent to have communicated the cessation of the wild Croatan Indians' violent spree in a less shocking way.

Had he been asked about this discrepancy between the unaltered image captured by his camera and the great ruckus that resulted from its having been seen, the photographer most probably would have mentioned that he'd been forced to wait until that very moment to capture the picture, his sense of propriety (not to mention the technical impossibility of composing a coherent image with all the motion going on) preventing him from taking a picture with children being posed by their parents in front of the open coffins or, as had been the issue the previous day, of including in the frame the group of debutantes picnicking beneath the hanging men, their laughter surely causing him as much discomfort as anyone seeing the image while reading a paper in the front room of their New York townhouse might have felt.

For many years after, that photograph represented the sum total of history's interest in the exploits of Edgar Seldom. Copies of it were sold for fifteen cents throughout North Carolina, East Tennessee, and in some places in the southwestern region of the Commonwealth of Virginia. They sold well until the early twentieth century, when an abbreviated summary of the outlaws' deeds printed on the back gave the pictures a small but temporary uptick in sales, though they were overtaken soon enough by other images of death: men in the long, winding graves of France, the light-pierced wrecks of bank robbers' getaway vehicles, and the autopsy pictures of dismembered film stars.

*   *   *

The summary on the back of the picture read as follows:

Indian bandits kill four officials in Robeson County
War against Confederates! 7 dead on border w/VA
Two conscription officers murdered in Durham.
Slaughter in Nansemond County: Injun Seldoms wipe
    out company of returning heroes!
Here lie the dead outlaws, killed in a shoot-out with
    brave lawmen.

Even as he rose up naked in the cool, waist-deep waters of the French Broad where he bathed, a ridiculous clump of suds clinging to his scarred shoulder and a fraction of a second before he was shot those fourteen times by the posse from the riverbank, Edgar thought of George. He breathed deeply of the free air, and readied himself to die with the certainty that he had done at least one good thing while on this poor, indifferent earth. Only a few of the posse members were ever willing to speak about the incident in the years that followed. One, Hank Jessup, swore that the ghost of Edgar Seldom visited him until the end of his days, which he spent as a greeter and volunteer at the Wonderland Hotel over in Sevier County, Tennessee, sometimes having to shake off a shudder when a vision of the young man's last smile arrived unexpectedly.

"I got to tell you, Mr. Seldom, we don't find too many folks looking for answers down here," Lottie said to George as he finished his breakfast and set it to the side.

He paused, wondering if he even knew the question he was hoping to find an answer to. "I just thought I might come down here and remember something," he said.

"Do you know where to look?"

"I remember a little. But it was so long ago. I don't even know if it would make a difference now." He laughed.

"Don't that depend on what you're hoping to find?"

"Sure," he said, "but it's all stuff you just can't put out in front of any old person."

"Come on now," Lottie said, feigning an affront, "don't go acting like I'm just anybody. If you came up down here it's likely we're some kind of kin. Most everybody around here is in one way or another. Who knows, my momma over there might know something. She's always in everybody's business."

"Well, that's just it," George began. "I was a foundling. Far as I can tell I ain't been kin to anybody in a good long while."

"Let's just say we're long-lost cousins. Don't know any different, do we? Maybe we can help."

"All right," George started, shifting in his seat. "I'm looking for a little cabin way back in a cypress grove along the Lumber. Lived there as a youngster with the woman who took me in. I don't know how to get there exactly, but I reckon it can't be too far."

"Sounds like a lot of places around here," Lottie said, "but it's something."

George went on, "You're too young to know it yet, and I don't mean to patronize, but when you get to be my age you see how your life just starts to fade away. And I don't mean at the edges, I mean right in the center of it. Sometimes seems like you wake up with no history, no connection to anything. Almost like amnesia, except you don't forget your name and all, just where you fit into a world that changes too fast to keep up with. So I remember little things, but I don't know why. And I remember big things, but I don't know why. Mostly I don't remember much of anything at all."

She reached over and picked up the rind of his unfinished toast but kept quiet.

George folded his hands in his lap and looked at the girl. "See, I used to watch the log drivers on their way to the Pee Dee and the lumber mills down in Georgetown near the coast. And I remember thinking, Anywhere but here. I got looked after pretty well, all things considered. But one day I just figured, That's where I'm going. And this woman, she treated me like her own, loved me like I was her own true son…"

"But?" Lottie asked.

"But I wasn't. It sounds silly now. Back then I would've swore it was the only thing that mattered. So one day I put some clothes in a little bag, hoofed it upriver to the logging show, and never looked back."

"She didn't want you to go."

George paused before answering. He rubbed his old beat-up hands inside each other. "I didn't ask. Didn't say a word of goodbye. Just up and left."

"I don't know much, Mr. Seldom," Lottie said. "But I'm sure you weren't the first to say 'Anywhere but here.' I say it once a day, and I know I won't be the last."

George smiled ruefully. They sat there together in silence for a while longer as he sank into memory. On the day he left he looked back from his perch on the log raft as the riverbanks disappeared into the cypress swamps. The breadth of black water covered in shadow even at midday. The sky blue and arcing above the clot of logs as the whole operation drifted downriver toward the Low Country. Rice extended beyond both banks of the river until there were two small green waves at each horizon. But for the stilted white winnowing barns, and the straw-hatted figures who came and went from them, hunched and stooping from their labor, George felt as though he was being carried through a vast, unexplored prairie. Beyond the prairie he imagined great cities walled up to heaven, but in truth he only found more wilderness. Soon enough, he could not even say where his home had been.

FIVE

BOB REID LOST his right arm in the Battle of Mechanicsville in June of '62. He had been a soldier in the Virginia Volunteer Dragoons for less than a year when he found himself
lying just above the swampy waterline of Beaverdam Creek
conversing with an enemy soldier, a Pennsylvanian named
Ernst Drahms, who had happened to fall close to, and soon
after, Bob. He could not remember exactly what had happened to him, only that he had lost a shoe in deep mud
somewhere between crossing the waist-high creek and running through tall grass toward the Federal lines and had
awoken some hours later assuming that he had been killed.

He mistook life for death on account of a curious illusion.
The sun was still out when he opened his eyes. All around
him the world buzzed and there was one tree standing by
itself in the green meadow between the trenches, and the
sound of the creek flowed in and out of the terrible hum
in his head. It seemed to him that he had been deposited
into Eden, or if not Eden, then he was getting a look at it
before he got there. He could even see his body a few feet

away from him, if we measure using distances occurring in the corporeal world, and he imagined passing away from it, not in ascension, but, still, a definite movement away, that he could be sure of.

In actual fact, the out-of-body experience he thought he had was only Bob's mind attempting to incorporate new information into its understanding of the world. The arm, which he had accurately identified as being the one to which his mind had always been married previously, was in reality no longer a part of his entire body. He had made the mistake of seeing his hand, the sleeve of his uniform, the unique arrangement of hair along the knuckles and above his wrist, and assuming, understandably, we might grant, that because it was oriented with the fingers pointing toward him and from several feet away, in a manner he would sometimes think of as accusatory later in his life, the rest of his body was still attached somewhere deeper into the grass beyond his ability to see, that his eyes ought to be looking out from and not into the wall of waving wild rye that hid whatever it was that existed beyond the elbow of his uniform.

He fixated on that spot in the tangle of bunchgrass for a while. Sensation returned, though slowly. Nausea overtook him in the evening, and he spent a while vomiting onto his own shoulder, discovering that movement had become a difficult proposition. He almost choked on it, once or twice, and he found it necessary to spit with all his might to keep from having these acidic expulsions return to fill his mouth and nose. His throat burned. Thirst returned. The sun fell beyond the trees. The sky darkened, hiding smoke on the wind from the chimney fires of nearby farms. Before full dark, Bob thought he recognized a pattern on the blades of grass. Some specks in shadow. Some wet black dew. He heard voices. Moans. The buzzing of a million flies.

Darkness on darkness. The night had a face. It knelt on his chest. Its weight pushed him deeper into the mud. Before it he felt only fear, as though his entire being had become a conduit for that one state. Distinctions fell away. He saw where he had been before his birth. The darkness there, too. A void broken only by spirals of color. A vastness so great as to be meaningless. The being he had not yet become spun through it helplessly.

He sat bolt upright, spat from the paralyzed terror of the void back into a simple, remorseless summer night on earth. His breathing was out of control, shallow and quick. He tried to raise himself up out of the mud only to collapse back into it face-first. The world became pain. Pain became the world. He sang an irreproducible song.

A voice spoke. It was close, near the tree line on the shoulder of ground above the creek bed where he had fallen that afternoon. "Friend," the voice called. "Friend! Are you dying?"

He tried to grab at the hand sticking out through the grass. He hung his head with exhaustion and looked down at the bloody mess below his right shoulder. He howled. "One of my arms is yonder in that grass," Bob yelled. "Believe my legs are broke, too."

Bob would never be privy to the exact sequence of events that led him to be lying, on speaking terms with death, in the grassy bed of a forgettable little creek outside Mechanicsville, Virginia, barely more than twenty miles from his home. All he'd ever remember is that he'd gotten his foot stuck in the mud after wading through the creek and charging toward the enemy lines. Almost parallel in time, a seventeen-year-old from Lancaster, Pennsylvania, pulled the string of his three-inch gun, which sent a projectile weighing approximately eight pounds toward the creek, across which streamed a line of whooping rebels that had until that moment included Sergeant Bob Reid of Chesterfield County. After successfully yanking his shoe out of the mud, he held it aloft with his right hand, and the projectile took his arm off somewhere between his elbow and shoulder. It would have been difficult to be more precise, due to the resulting damage. His legs were broken in multiple places over the next few minutes, trampled by a frantic mass of men and boys as they attacked and then retreated. He never saw the shoe again.

He waited for a few minutes, expecting a response from the voice that had called out to him. The mud he found himself in was the color of new brick and had a curious sheen in the moonlight. With his left hand he packed more mud onto the ugly protuberance below his right shoulder. There was still something uncanny about his arm being so close. The idea that it yet belonged to another man hidden in the tall grass did not leave him entirely and, in fact, never would.

"You still out there?" he called. He knew that he was not alone, for the little meadow was full of the sounds of suffering. Moans and grunts and calm, accepting sighs. Most of the screams had tapered off, the inevitable exhaustion of the human vocal cords being a thing toward which Bob began to feel a tremendous amount of gratitude. Soon he heard the noise of departure from the shoulder of the hill above him. Orders tersely barked. Wheels rolling over the rockier ground up there. Branches snapped and whipping in the dark.

The other voice came back. "Hear that ruckus? That would be the sound of my abandonment." The Federals were withdrawing.

"How you fixed over there? You need anything?" The last question made Bob ashamed, having forgotten the obvious need in which the dead and nearly dead found themselves, and that he was in no position to provide redress to any of the grievances this particular man would certainly have.

Bob heard the man emit a pitiful mixture of curses, moans, and laughter. "I've been stuck in my belly. Maybe shot, too. Hard to say. Got shit coming out where the blade went in. Can't be good." The man sighed. "I've cracked my glasses, too."

To his left, Bob heard the sound of two men grappling. Enemies that had fallen too close to each other and too alive to let things be. A cry of pain. A terrifying holler of triumph and relief. Daylight seemed to come no closer, as if the sun had the good sense not to shed its light on a scene so clearly belonging to the realm of night. He wished someone would light a fire, at least.

They agreed that it was better to talk than to try to kill each other. "Besides," the man said, "I think we will die soon either way." He learned the man's name in conversations long enough to require only a few breaths each. Ernst Drahms was a butcher in Lancaster, but he was originally from Hamburg. In 1842 his parents and siblings died in a fire that consumed much of the old city. He left for America with an overbearing, know-it-all uncle when he was seven. He did not remember much of his birthplace: a line of modest Lutheran spires painted in ash, the Elbe almost purple against the spits of sand and grasses at its estuary, a language left behind and then relearned in the hills and farms of central Pennsylvania.

"Can I tell you something funny, Bob?"

"Surely," he said.

"The man who owns the newspaper where I live paid me three hundred dollars to take his place. Maybe he'll have them write something nice about me." Bob didn't say anything. "I guess it's not really all that funny," said Ernst.

The night receded. Bob drifted in and out of consciousness. Before daybreak he heard a line of friendly skirmishers and litter bearers splash through the creek from the lines he'd left the day before. It was getting hot again already. No sign of rain. The air thick. He tried to call out to them, but his throat was so dry as to be sealed up. He heard them chattering around him. They lifted up a few groaning men and took them to the rear. He was almost stepped on by a boy who knelt down in the mud next to him and poked at his dirty face with his finger. "Shit fire!" the boy hollered. "Feller's still breathing here."

Bob croaked, "Water."

"We gonna get you fixed right up, mister, don't you worry." He poured a splash of water from his canteen onto a soiled rag and with it wet Bob's lips. Neither of them thought that he would live much longer. The boy then held his canteen up to Bob's mouth, gave him a drink, and sat down next to him. The litter bearers seemed to have quite a bit of work. It occurred to Bob that the boy was likely less than twenty years old. He had spots under the dirt caked on his face. The boy rifled through Bob's pockets. "Don't think you'll be needing all this, mister; you mind?" he asked. He took a tintype of Emily from inside Bob's coat pocket, held it up in the morning light, and said, "Kind of pretty, I guess. Pretty enough for my needs." He also took the last bit of Bob's coffee and a letter from Emily that the illiterate boy would use to wipe himself with after shitting in a ditch as the battle cascaded eastward a few days later.

The litter bearers finally arrived. They lifted him up and the howls he made were subhuman in nature, but didn't seem to bother anyone all that much. He wanted to ask them to grab his ring off the hand that was still resting in the grass, but found himself weeping, overcome with pain. As they took him away he watched the scavengers pick the pockets of the dead. He looked for Ernst. A few Federals lay dead or dying in the meadow. Bob could not be sure which body owned the voice that he had spoken to all night, but he guessed it was the man he saw at the bottom of the hill a few yards away. He wore dirty spectacles. He looked dazed but alive. The scavengers got to him first. They took something from his pockets. The boy who had found Bob removed Ernst's broken glasses and put them on his face. Blood speckled the lenses and painted the fractures in thin, dark lines of red. The German raised up his arms feebly. Bob watched from the unstable perch of his litter. *Don't do that,* he said to himself. *Don't do that!* he tried to call out louder. The boy looked back at Bob departing on the stretcher. "Don't give me that goddamn look," he said. The morning sun flashed in reflection. The scavengers then caved in Ernst's face, taking turns with the butts of their rifles. The impacts made a dull, thumping sound. They whooped and yelped. They danced their dance.

July was a dream. Visions and glimpses of visions. Bob was centered in the void most of the summer, though what he remembered of it when he woke in an airy ward of the Confederate hospital on Chimborazo Hill amounted to very little. Leaves dancing in the wind over the dusty roads of central Virginia. Maybe the noise of some river or another nearby. Heat unacquainted with the mercy of a breeze. Lucid for a two-day stretch in early August, he recalled waking with an itch on his right hand, but when he looked down the hand was still not there. Only a stump bandaged and covered over in plaster. But damn did it itch. When it did not itch, it hurt. Sometimes in the night he'd wake to clenched fists. He would let his left hand relax, but the ghost fist would not release, and the pain of it, seized up and indifferent to the direction of his mind, was a new torture.

He remembered the attendants bringing in a boy wounded at Cedar Mountain. They placed him in a cot across from Bob. Both legs mangled by grapeshot. The boy *had* both legs, more or less, thought Bob, but as to his feet, their presence was inconclusive. They gave the boy chloroform right before the operation began so there was no screaming; instead, for the next twenty minutes Bob listened to the sound of the surgeon scraping down the cutoff ends of his thigh bones to a flat, regular surface to ensure they would not push back through the skin after he was stitched up. Bob wished they'd have let the boy scream. Couldn't be worse than the noise that rasp made against the poor kid's bones.

In and out. Another run of unreliable consciousness. The stump began to stink. Out and in. The pain was almost gone by September, and Bob woke to mostly healed wounds. Soon he was well enough to send a letter. Though the hospital was less than a day's ride from his home in Chesterfield County, it took two weeks to receive a reply. Finally, Emily wrote to him:

Dear Father,

I am very sorry you were hurt. I want to come see you but Mr. Levallois says Richmond is too dangerous. Women riot in the streets for bread and the free negroes in Jackson Ward are telling every slave they meet that soon they, too, will be free. The lies. How can man undo what God himself has done? It is a terrible calamity and I pray for our people. Mr. Levallois came to see me often in early summer, some weeks he visited every day.

I can scarcely believe it has been so long since you left. More than a year? You looked very smart in your gray uniform and yellow kepi. I did not think you would be gone as long as this. After June, I received no answer to my letters. I thought you dead and wept for days. Mr. Levallois said that sometimes war is too much for a man, and if you deserted, not to judge you too harshly.

Mother is ill again and so is Aurelia. They are kept together in a sickroom at Beauvais. Mr. Levallois says it is best to keep me away from sickness. Another reason I cannot come to visit you, though I hope to see you again soon. He says the hospital is lousy with a thousand varieties of fever. Rawls looks after the mules and has kept some money coming in, minus what Mr. Levallois takes for renting him out to us. He is very generous.

Father, I fear the world is falling apart. Not even Champion around to bark from her lead on the sycamore. Some nights I have terrible dreams. We had our first autumn chill though it is only September and tomorrow Mr. Levallois is sending Rawls to make me a cord of firewood. I went to see Mother in her sickroom but could only speak to her from behind the door. Her voice was very weak. I am so afraid for her. What will become of us after this terrible war? I so want things to go back to the way they were before. Do you think they will? Mr. Levallois offered me the use of his overseer's house so I would not be so lonely. He says solitude and troubles do not mix. The overseer was killed at Seven Pines so his house is empty. When Mother and Aurelia are well again Mr. Levallois says I am to take a room in the big house.

Your dutiful child,
Emily

Weeks more would pass before he walked again, and even then he required the aid of a cane and a leg brace with no less than a dozen parts fully assembled. Such pity accompanied his afternoon constitutionals that he began to feel outwardly monstrous. Mothers on the sidewalks of Church Hill whisked their children out of sight. Even the slaves in the cookhouse averted their eyes when he neared, though Bob never realized that this was due to the lifelong understanding among them that nothing existed in God's great wide world more dangerous than a white man feeling sorry for himself.

A slave girl assisted him in his outings. Though Bob did not know it, she was rented to the hospital at such a generous rate that its commandant had given her master, Mr. Levallois of Beauvais Plantation, a silver-plated ceremonial pistol engraved with the words DEO VINDICE as a gesture of appreciation. Had Bob realized his strange connection to the girl, he might have succumbed much earlier to the paranoia that would eventually overtake him after his return to Chesterfield.

*   *   *

Nurse did not speak to Bob when she was first assigned his convalescence. In fact, she rarely spoke at all unless out of absolute necessity. At the Devil's Half Acre, she was taught a language beyond speech, one that existed when the ground on which all her torments occurred had been submerged below a channel sea, with a vocabulary that remained unchanged even with the unending forces of thrust and rift at work. From her cell she had seen the rending of the earth, mountains form and then subside and form again, the decay of all things made by God made permanent; animal, vegetable, mineral; the inner workings of the globe condensed down to one fixed point on its topography that she confused, forgivably, with a place outside of time. The tumult of the planet spoke to her in one sentence, said over and over again for a year and a half, the pitiless seasons passing outside on Wall Street, in a voice that took the form of a door creaking, boot heels on a stone floor, and a candle held aloft as it approached the darkness of the whipping room. No, she had learned the language of eternity, and she would not sully herself again with words white men had forced into her mouth if it could be helped.

A man named Mr. Levallois bought her from Lumpkin for a song in the summer of 1862. She had not eaten in weeks. Lumpkin thought she would be dead soon, so when the dark-haired man offered him a reasonable price for her, she was sold immediately. Mr. Levallois did not say why he'd bought her, only that he had heard what happened to her from her former master and he wanted to offer her a bargain. "Go work at the hospital awhile," he said, "and I will do something for you in return." She did not answer him. "You would rather die here?" he asked. Nurse was silent. "I always try to be reasonable," he said, "but sometimes you niggers don't understand. You cannot even die unless I allow it. All that you have been and all that you will ever be, I own." She did not want to work at the hospital. She had no desire to help those wounded men get back to a war that, if won, would bring down a plague on her people of such duration and intensity that even her visions in the whipping room at Lumpkin's Jail could not have encompassed it. All hope of deliverance abandoned. Mr. Levallois came to see her every day the week after he bought her. She was still at the jail, but she had been moved from the pens into a plain, clean room. The trips to the whipping room ended. Sometimes he came during the day and he would ask her if she had changed her mind. Sometimes he came at night and did not ask anything. She did not understand why this man insisted on her assent when it was not required for him to do as he pleased, but she felt that giving it to him would mean giving away something she might not ever get back. Perhaps, she thought, that is what he was after in the first place. When three more nights passed in the same way she reached a new depth of numbness she had not known before. The next time he entered the room, she spoke. "I'll go to the hospital. If you'll leave me be, I'll go."

When she arrived by carriage at Chimborazo that summer, she had very little hope. And though the hope she did have was small, every day it was slightly tended to and nourished as she walked through the pavilions listening to the men and boys bleating like filthy hogs on their way to the abattoir. She recalled the celebrations and send-offs at the beginning of the war so clearly, mere months after her imprisonment at Lumpkin's Jail. The Devil's Half Acre was right in the heart of Richmond. In fact, it *was* the very beating heart of Richmond. And from it Nurse heard a great variety of goings-on. Horns blaring in the squares. The robust youth that passed in disorderly formation that first spring following her imprisonment, their gray uniforms a slow stream that wound down Main Street toward the docks. And now here they were after just over a year of war, four thousand of them arranged in rows, shitting themselves, their gangrenous limbs stinking and useless, many of them dead already, some knowing and some not, as helpless as the firstborn of Egypt without a drop of blood above their doors.

Nurse knew Bob Reid only by name when she saw him that September. But by overhearing the doctors' talk, and listening to the man's own fevered ramblings, she eventually concluded that this was the very same man who owned Rawls and his mother, who owned the mules Rawls worked, who owned the land from which he ran toward their meeting place among the loblolly, before her mistress fell off her horse and died, before she was sent to Lumpkin's. The first day she arrived at his bedside she cleaned his face with a damp sponge. He passed into and out of delirium. She wanted to ask about Rawls, but since one never knew where trouble would come from she did not. Instead she hinted at deafness when he spoke to her so that she would not have to reply to his muttering. Day upon day. The man wept regularly, not out of pain, Nurse did not think, but from the now-undeniable nature of his enfeeblement.

Nurse arrived at Bob's bedside at nine o'clock each morning. It took her twenty minutes to affix the brace to his right leg, the one that had suffered the worst of his trampling. He regained something like lucidity by October; though it was accompanied by a bitterness that Nurse was sometimes afraid would reach out and grab her by the throat. He stared at her as she tightened screws and worked the wooden pieces of the leg brace into place. His green eyes followed her from his expressionless face. He had grown a beard during his time in the hospital that accentuated the gauntness of his wrecked body. She combed his hair and swung his legs off the side of the bed. Into his left hand she placed a cane after dressing him, and with much effort pulled him to his feet.

Bob breathed deeply as the girl lifted him up. He tested the strength of the cane, letting his weight collect on it very slowly, until he felt it could bear all remaining 136 pounds of him. The testing had become a habit, a ritual, really, because he had already refused to be attended to by his previous nurse, a lovely enthusiastic volunteer from Fluvanna County, after she had seen him fall helplessly to the filthy wood floor of his forty-man ward. The fall had not been the girl's fault, but Bob became so obsessed with his own shame that he started to hate her; her smiling freckled face, the genuine encouragement she tried to offer that seemed to Bob an unbearable form of condescension. The girl's slender, youthful body, the outline of which was sometimes visible in the morning light under her bloody garments, tormented him, though it would be difficult to say whether Bob's fixation was out of unconsummated lust or because of the wholeness and absence of injuries he knew her body to possess.

Some mornings Bob would say to Nurse, "You mock me, girl?" and she would smile bashfully as if she did not understand until he let the question go. They walked circuits through and around the pavilions at first, until some of his strength returned. They widened their route in November, passing St. John's Church on a blanket of yellow leaves above the cobblestones. Nurse had to steady him still, and often, and one day Bob looked at her with frustration, being in the curious position of needing her to remain upright while at the same time despising her necessity. "You mock me, girl. I can tell. You pity me like all the rest."

Nurse felt intense joy in that moment. For once it seemed as though she had permission from the world to tell the truth, a condition so rare in her life she had nearly thought it impossible. "No, Mr. Reid," she said softly, "I do not pity you. I do not pity any of you. And I swear I never will."

Bob looked at her briefly, trying to decide whether this was honesty or impertinence, and allowed her to steady him for the first time without resentment. "I thought you were deaf and dumb" was all he said. "All right, then. Let's keep going."

The air was cold that day on the hills above the city. Clouds blackened the sky. The screams of patients barely reached them from the amputation tents, but reached them still. It began to rain. Before Nurse led Bob back to his ward, they passed a pile of discarded limbs, legs and arms, perhaps a hundred or more. Some of them still bled. Toes kicked at the sky above the mud, stupidly. The pile reached the angle of repose. If unmolested, it could have sat there like a monument until the bones were bleached white by the sun over a hundred thousand summers. Until they became nothing more than a white particulate streak in the sediment. Until this whole place sat forgotten again beneath the shallow channel sea she sometimes swam in in her dreams. Nurse saw Bob to his bed and returned to her quarters, passing by the amputation tent again. Agony, then quiet, but never silence. No, there would not be silence in this place for many years. An orderly came out of the tent and tossed a ruined leg onto the pile. The whole assemblage collapsed. Nurse shook her head at the scene. And here I am a child of God, she thought.

By the time winter came Nurse knew how the war would end. In the evenings, after her duties ended, she would go out to the eastern edge of the hill and watch a line of crowded hearses roll slowly into darkness toward Oakwood Cemetery. As her breath froze on the air, and she pulled her shawl tight around her shoulders, she tallied up the dead. She knew how many might fit into one wagon, could count the wagons as they left the hospital, and could figure how many might have taken their loads in daylight while she attended to her duties. Soon others gathered with her there. One or two might come from the cookhouse and stand quietly as they watched torches flicker in the distance as the gravediggers went about their work.

"What do you think will happen to us when they figure out they've lost?" asked one of the cooks. The question startled Nurse. She realized she had not yet allowed room in her heart for after. Another man explained to the assembled group that he had been rented out to the Confederate army just a few hours before Union cavalry overran his master's house out on the Middle Peninsula. He told them that the last he'd seen of his master, he and the overseer were herding the unrented slaves into the barn. Eight of them had been deemed unable to contribute to the cause. Two men born in the last century, when the songs of the Mattaponi dances were heard by nearby slaves in the waving green oceans of tobacco, calmly led the remaining six—a five-year-old girl, twin boys not yet weaned from their mother, a pair of ageless women, and the mother of the children—into the barn. There was no need for the cook to explain that the fire came next, though it is what happened. His hands were so weighed down by his shackles that he could not raise them up to cover his eyes, which in that moment was his only desire. So he shut them tightly against the glow beyond the pines and listened to a single shot ring out.

"Five thousand since I've been here," she said.

"Hmm," the man grumbled in reply.

"In this one place. Think of it. Soon enough there will be no one left to fight."

"How soon is soon enough is what I want to know. Lincoln says we free now, but you know what'll happen if I go tell master I'm going back to my people out in Middlesex," the man said.

Of course Nurse knew. And she did not care what people said, except for the fact that new words being said can sometimes create a new record to measure deeds against. No, she cared what people did. Sadly, what they did was talk most of the time. But now Yanks were killing graybacks by the bushel. That's doing. Nurse saw the gravediggers' torches bobbing closer now. The burials ended for the moment. The men trudged along the path leading them back up the eastern slope of Chimborazo Hill and back to their quarters.

"Someday I will join the free folks in Great Dismal," the man said quietly. "Someday I will find those islands and live like God intended."

Nurse rubbed her belly. It was undeniable. It had been for a good long while. Soon enough she'd show no matter how heavy her clothes were. She wondered what kind of cursed life could have been conceived in that room with Levallois at the Devil's Half Acre. She was no longer numb. The little one had started kicking. But sorrow had not yet made room for joy inside her heart. Maybe it would open the door someday, if not wide enough for joy then perhaps wide enough for light. She did not know but hoped. That night she dreamed outside of time again. She floated along the narrow avenues between the wards of canvas and clapboard. All empty. The earth was dry and the sun was warm.

The tents had been rolled up and a pleasant breeze blew through the canvas, now clean and free of blood and grime. The whole world smelled of apple-cider vinegar and a good hard scrub. She found the last of her patients in a small tent and led them by their hands to a waiting hearse. Their graves waited for them, too. They lay down in the shallow voids, expressionless, as she took up a gleaming shovel and covered them. All the men in gray were dead, from Westmoreland on the Potomac to Glorieta Pass, from Tullahoma to Mobile, Alabama. She was overcome with a sense of finality and permanence. In the dream she thanked God for the great privilege of life. The next day Bob asked her half-a-dozen times why she would not stop smiling. She did not answer. But neither did she stop.

SIX

LATE MORNING. George slept in the booth in the diner, his head propped against the sunny window on a stack of folded aprons brought by Lottie not long after their talk subsided and he began to snore. He had joked earlier about the young woman's lack of experience, but he knew she was old enough to have had her share, and if not, that did not mean she was too young to see what was coming. And though he had not come down here to be a burden in his passing, should it come to that, he surely understood that consequences care only a little for intention or desire.

It seemed to Lottie that the man slept peacefully, and she began to feel an unexamined warmth toward him that is not uncommon among the young toward the old. And though he did not seem frail in any obvious way, she felt the need to ask her mother if they ought not ask a doctor to come check on him while he dozed.

"He's settling up with God, Lottie," her mother said, "but that doesn't mean anything's coming due today."

Lottie did not reply, but continued watching the old man

with a mixture of curiosity and care. "You think something's wrong with him, though?" she asked.

Her mother simply put her hand on Lottie's dark unblemished cheek, said, "Sure there is. Same thing as everybody else, hon," and turned away.

Lottie leaned back against the window glass, warming her back and shoulder blades in the near-noon sun. She crossed her legs and let her feet dangle out over the edge of the booth and lit a cigarette, which she held in her left hand. With her right hand, she reached across the table toward Mr. Seldom, not to touch him, only so that she might be nearer should it somehow be the thing that made a difference. She closed his book and let her hand rest on its worn cover.

With George asleep, the diner went on in its characteristic quiet. On most days, a dinner rush might consist of two people who had taken a wrong turn and stopped to ask for directions. The chatter of the cooks smoking out back on their upturned milk crates only reached them when a hot wind pushed open the broken door. The bell would ding, and Lottie and her mother would turn to see the door close again behind the retreating breeze.

"Don't you think we ought to help him?" Lottie said.

"You mind your business, young lady," her mother answered.

Lottie smiled at her playfully. "Of all people to say such a thing…"

"Very funny." Her mother looked at the sleeping man and went on, "I don't recall hearing him ask us for help. Besides, what are you gonna do, give him a piggyback ride? You don't know where he's trying to go, and you don't have a way to get there if you did. You want to know what I think?"

"I bet you're gonna tell me either way," said Lottie.

Her mother wagged her finger at her and said, "You're just bored and want to cut out of work early. You think I don't know my own daughter?"

"I know, I know," Lottie said a little too earnestly. "How are you gonna handle all these customers without me?"

Her mother folded her arms and shot her a look of concern. "You trust too much, Lot. The world won't always love you back." Lottie started to object, but her mother continued, "You go on. I've got to get your daddy from work later, but I'll bring the car back to the house in a few hours. You can take it if you don't stay out too late. And don't wander too far from home. Nothing good will ever come from that."

When George woke a short time later, Lottie's hand was still near to him, her cigarette smoke reminded him of a fire in a hearth, and he smiled through a yawn.

Whatever he meant to find down here, thought Lottie, he would not be going back to Virginia without it. Either it would be found or not, but here. Lottie told George what she'd come up with while he'd slept. She'd gotten an inkling of where they might start. Lottie knew of a few places along the river where old cabins still stood in the depths of the swamp. She told George they could drive east toward Lumberton to see if there was anything out there that matched his memories.

To Lottie, the day was now endowed with possibility. As

they left the diner and stood in the parking lot, she said excitedly, "You want to see a movie? I've seen it twice already, but I don't mind seeing it again." George could see how eager she was and said, "Sure. I can't recall the last time I went to see a picture."

They walked toward town and entered the theater around three o'clock, a few minutes before the curtain rose, ascending the staircase marked CROATAN slowly enough that George was only slightly winded when they sat down beyond the rope strung across the far corner of the balcony. The picture was *Shane,* and George could plainly see that Lottie was giddy in her seat.

As the opening newsreels began in the projector's first bright light, all silver and swirling black, a voice described a fleet of bombers encircling the world. They would use, if necessary, roads as runways, and George recognized one of these depicted on the reel. From an aerial view, perhaps shot from the belly of one of these great flying beasts, the cavernous gash through Jackson Ward appeared. It seemed to him not unlike a wound in the city of Richmond itself, a hole so vast its bottom would be at best theoretical. The angle changed and a man stood before the ruins of the ward, his hand swept up as if the scope of the destruction required gesticulation as accompaniment, and yet his voice spoke only of triumph as the crew and equipment disappeared from view, descended finally into the unseen depths to contend with bedrock.

He did not know when the footage had been shot, but the scope and scale of the alterations to the neighborhood he'd known as home for many years were irrevocable. It occurred to him that even the landmarks of his plain, uninteresting life were almost unrecognizable when mediated by the sweeping cinematic shots and the enthusiastic confidence of the reporter's voice. There was a brief period, a moment of apprehension, when he thought perhaps all this erasure had occurred in another Richmond, another south, on a far unmapped side of the world, and that if he retraced his steps, asked the girl to put him on the Greyhound back to Fayetteville, rode the train northward toward Virginia over the endless strands of the great bay's thousand rivers, he would find his home unchanged, Leona tall and dark and beautiful, smiling at him without resentment or regret for their childlessness as he pulled the Zephyr to the curb and let the Motorola play some song she loved, and the ward would bustle as a lived-in place should. But no, I am an exile again, he thought. A wound as deep as the sea, just as Henry Levy had said. Behind the reporter, he saw a house that looked very much like the one he'd lived in with his wife, and then alone after he'd buried her at Oakwood, and had finally abandoned mere hours before they tore it down. When he'd bought the house, with a mortgage from St. Luke Penny Savings in the neighborhood, he stayed up all night for a week peering out the curtains, waiting for someone to take it away from him. Finally, so many years later, they had come. In the footage, a man emerged from the door of the house. He stood on the porch and leaned out over the chasm. He wore a white suit in the footage and was likely not intended to be captured by the camera, but nevertheless was. George wondered what rummaging had gone on, what the workmen might have scavenged from his home, if what had been precious to him had been handled with derision and contempt, perhaps a child's unused baptismal gown on the smallest hanger in his closet, or a picture of his late wife in an unguarded moment. He knew the answer, of course. In some places, and at some times, no distinction between public and private life is allowed. You might as well be put out naked in the street. And while he did not know the extent of this exposure, he did not think this fact qualified as mercy.

A few folks had been given payments for their homes, though even these were cruelly absurd in their distance from what the market would have declared appropriate. For the rest of his neighbors, a declaration of eminent domain compounded their powerlessness. Over the following months they watched the wreckage of their homes as the debris was trucked from the open mouth of the construction site toward the landfills along Jeff Davis Highway. All this was witnessed from the windows of their newly assigned apartments in Gilpin Court, on the northern border of the construction site, poorly built and soon forgotten, from which they would turn away so as not to be reminded further that the old order changes not.

George knew the story, though he had not seen the picture nor heard much about it, except that Jack Palance had apparently given a strong turn as the villain. He knew the story because he had heard it said that really there are only two kinds: one in which a hero goes on a journey, the other in which a stranger comes to town. He smiled and Lottie looked over at him and he shifted in his seat, adopting an attentive posture so she would know his mood should not be mistaken for a dismissive attitude toward the movie she had chosen. He was smiling because it occurred to him that maybe there was really only one story; suppose the hero on his journey winds up as a stranger in your town?

After the movie ended it began to rain. They stood under the small marquee and waited, hoping that the storm would pass so they could get the car. George felt himself wheeze a bit, and though it was a summer storm, he instinctively pulled the collar of his light jacket tight. Lottie acted out scenes on the sidewalk, turning her hands into pistols and shooting everything in sight, like only someone who has never seen one fired outside of the movies can do. Lottie gushed about Alan Ladd on horseback, his skill with a gun, the boy shouting for him to come back, but George thought his character responsible for the consequences that befell all involved, that he had a delusional nature. And anyway, though he agreed Ladd was as good in parts as Lottie said, he was also disappointed, because George couldn't shake the feeling that Ladd was afraid of horses, and he was sure he saw him flinch whenever his gun went off.

Palance's was the performance he really admired. There was honesty in it. Whoever said a rifle on a wall was an opportunity for suspense must have been European. As if there would ever be a question of its getting fired or not in America. The gun goes off when the line gets crossed, and the line got crossed a long time ago, when we were naked and wandered the savanna and slept beneath the baobab trees. *When* is simply a matter of how long it takes to get it out of the holster, how long it takes the bullet to arrive. Perhaps days or weeks or months, perhaps one's whole life, but these are questions of distance and trajectory, of time and physics, and not of possibility. George thought Palance must be an actor of rare talent, because those dark, pin-pricked eyes told the truth at the heart of every story, that violence is an original form of intimacy, and always has been, and will remain so forever.

George never carried a gun himself. There were times he wished he had in the immediate and unnavigable anger he sometimes found himself in at inexplicable moments, but to be who he was in the places and times through which he lived made the prospect difficult. To pick up a pistol and hold it in a hand that looked like his, well, it could be said he might as well put the barrel against his head and save the middlemen the trouble. And so even as a much more robust man than the one who sat in the theater and watched Alan Ladd kill the only honest man in the whole damn movie, he carried nothing but his delicate knife with the handle of elk antler to protect himself. He never used it to that end, though he remained ready to do so if the need arose. He had no interest in martyrdom, or in turning either cheek, and valued peace less than his life, but this is not to say George regarded life as precious generally, or that if he did he was uniquely perceptive to it. He was not particular in that way. He was sure only that his life ought to belong to him. And he was content to let other men determine what that value might be if they had the starch to pay what it would cost to take it from him, from those hands of his so suited to bringing down with a swinging blade that which nature had taken a hundred years or more to raise. Those were the terms the world had offered him, and so he did his best to keep his ledger balanced, and to worry less about that unknowable cost than what he might be paid for a hard day's work.

The knife was in the back pocket of his dungarees when he put Great Dismal behind him for good in the wake of Huggins's death, not realizing he was retracing his steps more closely than he could have wished those many years later when he arrived alone in Pembroke at the end of his life. He headed south and east toward the Outer Banks at the tail end of a distant February, first riding a log-laden barge to the terminus of the swamp's canal in the town of South Mills just on the other side of the North Carolina border. He then walked for two days and nights along the edges of dirt roads not yet having to resist their being buried by the wild growth of the coastal plains in spring. When he arrived at Camden Courthouse, he smelled the winter sea, though he could not see it yet. It was dusk and the Pasquotank River drained into the sound through a line of drowned trees. The lights of Elizabeth City on the river's western shore inspired in him a feeling he could not name. It was not nostalgia, nor wistfulness, nor longing, but there was a bit of melancholy in it, though George acknowledged that this was the terrain many of his feelings were native to. And though the past surely played a part, he had never been to Elizabeth City, so it was not a place he missed or had ever even hoped to see. But the feeling bore a curious resemblance to contentment, too, and he slept soundly after watching the lights go out one by one, curled into his coat next to the dying embers of a fire, listening to the wind and the waves and the ringing of the buoy bells.

In the morning he carried Huggins's belongings to the dock in a pack slung over his shoulder and boarded a boat bound for the village of Kitty Hawk on Bodie Island. The knife lay next to an orange bandanna with which he wiped his brow from time to time when pausing to look out over the sound and the sea grass along the banks. One of the items in the pack was a letter bearing the address of Huggins's people. He worried that to read it would be intrusive, even though Huggins could not object, buried as he was in a patch of artificially high ground near the logging camp George had left behind forever.

In those days an address carried a different kind of specificity. It required the deliverer to have some knowledge of the destination beyond the rigorously systematic arrangement by which people, in later years, would fool themselves into thinking that a name and number constituted an accurate description of a place. And so George looked at the envelope on which was written in a delicate, faded cursive, *Go north from Kitty Hawk toward Corolla, two houses past Douglas Slough's dock on the sound side, the yellow one, but not yet to the place you can see the lighthouse from.* With that as his guide after landing, George set off to tell the young man's people that their son Huggins would not be coming back, and to perhaps console them if the news he carried did not make such a proposition impossible.

He walked several miles along the edge of the Atlantic Ocean, passing a rescue station and a few hotels shuttered for winter, before stopping for the night. He did not know how far he had to go yet, but he had walked all day through the sand, stopping often to watch the banker ponies graze on wind-whipped cordgrass and gallop through the rising gray tide. He slept in the dunes where the ribbon of sand seemed at its thinnest, not even a hundred yards wide, and he felt an unusual claustrophobia after nightfall when the vastness of both sea and sound were swallowed by a darkness immune to human measurement. He was glad to be out of the wind, though, and eventually the claustrophobia passed and instead with the stars and the water's constant roar came a sense that everyone on earth was irrelevant, that if the world were emptied of people tomorrow they would not be missed at all, not by bird nor beast, or God up in heaven or the devil down in hell. It took a bit of getting used to, but he was surprised how comforting it was to feel that this was so.

He found the house quite easily the following afternoon. Though inefficient, the address was accurate, and when he saw the redbrick spire of the lighthouse through the pines, he turned around, confident that he was close. After a few more minutes of searching he found himself in the Hugginses' dooryard. A rooster strutted across the sandy ground, and he saw a pen behind the house in which two sturdy horses trotted casually. He knocked on the door. A man not much older than George opened it. The man had the Down East way of speaking, which surprised him a little, as Huggins had been so free of accent in his speech that it must have required a great effort for him to get that way. His father, on the other hand, spoke with a sound as thick as the center of a marsh, and George could not understand much of what was being said at first, though when the man waved him in and said, "Mother, some woodser come and want to talk," he followed. They sat around a table. George looked through the window and out past the scrub and cattails where the sound was still as stone, and the winter sun did little to distinguish the gray sky from the water below it. He told them what had happened to their son, that he had been a fine young man and a good worker. The woman got up from the table and walked toward the back door.

"Drime," she said.

"She don't believe it," the man said.

"I'm sorry."

"I told the boy, 'High tide on the sound side. Nothing for you there. Work to do yet here. A good thing to have work to do.' But he thought he were something special. Would even say so, a hurtful thing because it's telling everyone else they ain't."

George began to say that he was sorry again, but held it back, and instead placed his knapsack on the table and removed Huggins's things from it one by one. There was a notebook, in which George recognized the delicate cursive from the unopened letter, and then the letter itself, which Huggins's father tucked immediately into his shirt pocket. There was also a small driftwood carving of a fishing trawler that had fishing line strung from the mast and crane as a gesture toward mechanical accuracy. He took out the boy's clothes and became embarrassed because his own had gotten mixed in with them.

With the objects finally arrayed on the table it seemed astonishing to George that even a short life could leave so little behind. But he silently acknowledged that from his own there would be even less.

"So that's it, then," the man said.

"I suppose it is," said George.

Outside the small house they heard his mother crying, and they looked at each other as if to say that they hoped the other might be able to do something about it. But there was nothing to be done that time could not do better. The look on the father's face changed. He rose from his chair and went to get his coat from where it hung on a peg next to the doorframe. George thought he sensed the man's desire to be alone, but he was mistaken, for what he sensed was the man's terror of exactly that.

George followed him out. They walked to the rear of the yard where the horses pawed distractedly at the ground. The horses were not tall, and had low-set tails, but were broad and healthy like the ponies George had seen running along the shore. The man hitched them to a cart and slapped the seat next to his, and George sat down beside him. The woman had gone inside already, but they could hear her weeping still, even over the noise of the wooden wheels rolling over the rock-hard sand.

"It's me who Mother'll think done it," he said.

The day had warmed up some. The sun broke through the clouds and lit up the ocean with a blue-green light as they rode along it heading south.

"To tell the truth," George said, "if it was anyone, it was me. I was struck ill a while back and it was me and Hug working together generally. But I was laid up. He might have listened if I'd been there. Or done something or not done some other thing. I don't know."

"Well, that won't suit Mother, I'll tell you. She'll fix it on me, and you'll just upset her further if you make her work at it. See, the boy was not nobody that ought to have made big plans, but Mother says I speak too much about my disappointments, and I give the boy the notion that we have some say in the matter."

George did not respond. But he understood.

"And so it would not matter one lick to her if I was at fault for his leaving, or his staying, or his not coming back. They's all rolled up in one parcel."

It seemed unusual for a man to speak so openly about his life, especially down south where you'd get to know about a person best when they were not around and someone else was left to do the telling. The changes of the last thirty or forty years had been hard on the people out there on the far edge of America. The man told him how his family's trade had been in scavenging, and that in his father's youth a man could feed his family from it. How he'd go down to Cape Point, hang a lantern from a horse's neck, and lead the horse up and down the beach. The bob of the light in the darkness would look to sailors like just another ship at sea, and once in a while they'd bust their hull up on the Wimble Shoals. The Gulf Stream would put the sailors on the beach a while later, and his father would then push his dinghy in the water to collect what the sea had not wanted for itself.

"Was the shoals did it. I know what you woodsers think. But you can't eat sand, and there's only so much fish, so we took what the shoals give." He paused. "I guess a feller thinks he needs to outdo his father."

"I expect that's true," said George.

But those days were gone, and though the man was nostalgic for them, he reluctantly admitted it was for the best. "Man can drown in a puddle. Best not help it along when most folks will get there on their own in due time." He asked George to keep his eyes open for anything along the beach that looked like it did not belong. George replied that he had seen the ocean for the first time just the day before and that he was not sure he would know what belonged or not. "That's all right," he said. "If it suits your eye, it'll be just fine for the dingbatters at the hotel this summer."

Back at the house they sat around the cooking stove and sorted through their scraps. There was enough variety that the summer crowd might believe they'd found Blackbeard's buried treasure in a wreck, as Mr. Huggins aimed to tell them.

They asked George if he wanted to stay with them awhile.

He accepted. As easily as they shared their home and lives with him, his willingness to be equally open came more slowly. For obvious reasons, but also perhaps because his disposition required caution in matters such as these, George was free with gratitude, and assistance, and labor of all kinds, but not with affection, and less so with his history. "He's a stoic, Mother," the man would say. George would only smile without opening his mouth, and wonder why he felt that delivering the fateful message to them about their son's accidental death had transformed into the repayment of a debt. And he did not know it at the time, but their greatest act of kindness was to allow him to repay that debt, though they knew quite well by then that George Seldom did not owe the world a thing.

SEVEN

LATE ONE EVENING, not long after Bob Reid watched his life float off in the smoke and haze above the little muddy creek outside Mechanicsville, Rawls returned to Beauvais and entered the study. He found Levallois with a pipe going and a single candle illuminating the week-old copy of a northern paper from which his master looked up at him. "What is it?" he asked.

"I'm thinking Mr. Reid's place is 'bout to go bust and he ain't here to do nothing about it."

"Hmm." Levallois chewed on the end of his pipe for a moment before snapping at the newspaper with the backs of the first two fingers of his right hand. "It says here that the British have annexed an island in Africa. And France has absorbed three provinces in the Orient. What do you make of that?"

"I don't know."

"All their talk of freedom, all their sanctimony. Man doesn't return to the jungle without a reason."

"I suppose you're right, sir."

"And what of Reid?"

"Hardly any freight to tote down to the docks."

Levallois stood and stretched and paced over to a mirror hanging above the fireplace mantel. "Hardly any freight," he repeated quietly. "And you have a theory as to why?"

"No theory. Fact as fact can be."

"Well, let loose with it." Levallois saw Rawls in the mirror eyeing the club chair opposite the one from which he had risen. Between the chairs stood a small marble table and a decanter of brandy. He looked down in the reflected darkness to where Rawls shifted his weight from one foot to the other in a predictable rhythm of habit and discomfort. He thought of the ignorant soybean peddler who had tried to ruin such a valuable asset. But he then considered the fact that he really owed Rawls's former owner a debt, that so much of what Levallois had been given had come his way through the inability of other men to find value in unexpected places, or to realize that desire, unlike pain, was something that no one, black or white, would ever develop a resistance to while the sun still sat as center of the heavens. He saw Rawls grimace ever so slightly in the mirror, a look that Rawls deftly and comfortably converted to a sly smile. He almost felt sorry for the boy but did not. Levallois gave his gifts rarely, and never without calculation. "Sit and talk with me like a freeman would," he said, keeping his gaze into the mirror's silver waves.

Rawls moved toward the chair, then paused only long

enough for it to be perceptible to Levallois. He smiled and returned to his chair. He then poured out two snifters and motioned for Rawls to continue.

"Time was folks could only get their goods down the docks on the narrow gauge. As you know, that time's many years gone. No one has to go as far to load up. And once they get loaded, the new line will get your freight farther for a lot less money. For a good long while after, folks would find cause to gripe about the new rail lines, costs and such, and how much they preferred the old ways."

"I see," he said. He poured Rawls another drink, which he tipped back as quickly as he had the first. "Slowly," Levallois said.

"No one gripes about the old ways anymore," Rawls said. "The new ways just became the old ways without anyone seeming to notice but me."

Levallois put his glass down on the tabletop and nearly ran over to a standing desk above which hung a framed Mercator map. Rawls did not immediately recognize what it depicted, as he had never seen a map encompassing the entirety of the globe. He listened to the scratch of pen on paper in the low light and poured himself another drink. Levallois stood over Rawls a moment later. The dull glow of the fire and the spitting candle reduced the library to its essential elements: the room, the two men, the table and chairs, all inside an abyss of competing shadows. Rawls felt dizzy and warm and a little nauseated. Levallois handed him an envelope. "Take this to my bank tomorrow. Get the lawyer on your way back." He poured Rawls another drink. "You're one of the good ones, Rawls. I knew it when I first saw you in that field."

Rawls felt as though all his troubles had ended. The brandy coursed through his veins in a now-uncomplicated world. He could not remember pain or heartache. He did not miss Nurse the way he always did. "I don't understand, Mr. Levallois," he said, beginning to slur his words.

Levallois smiled. "People can be relied upon so well to show you the right course if only you want to see it."

Rawls's eyes fluttered. He soon would sleep. The following morning, he would forget to say that it would be a hard day, and tomorrow even harder. But the world would remember on his behalf. "Sir?" he muttered.

"I've been looking for a sign, Rawls. Waiting for one. I did not know what to do, but you have shown me. So I now must relieve another man of the burden of that which he is not equal to," said Levallois.

He fetched a quilt from another downstairs room and laid it over Rawls. Levallois occasionally allowed for acts like these to be mistaken for kindness. He hoped that Rawls would come to love him for them. But he did not believe in kindness. He believed in fulfilling destinies, and that his was to be among the rare men who clearly saw the earth and everyone who walked on it stripped of their ridiculous pretensions. He rolled his head around his neck and felt the bones pop methodically. I am a mechanism in a great machine, he thought. I am truly a servant to those who cannot serve themselves.

*   *   *

The following day Rawls staggered through a hangover, out from the shade of Beauvais's veranda, and into the bright sun. There had been no word at all from Reid at that point, and Rawls agreed with his master that Reid was likely dead. The war had picked up its pace, and the killing had picked up as a consequence. On most nights nowadays Rawls went to sleep to the boom of cannon fire to the north and east. He woke to it as well, with the tumult closer each morning than it had been the night before. Beyond that, it was not his place to question. Rawls heard the lawyer tell Levallois that it was only a matter of time until everything would be settled as he wished. To Rawls, his master only said that there was no reason to wait for the inevitable, and then gave him his instructions.

He got the rig together and rode toward the Reid place with a team of men bouncing in the back as the cart slalomed between the drive's deep ruts. Rawls slowed as they passed the overseer's house. He removed his hat when he saw Emily standing on the porch watching them as they headed toward the road. She studied them intensely, and without prompting Rawls called out to her, saying, "Mr. Levallois had him a deal go through. Got us doing some sorting out on it."

Emily took the steps down to the drive. She had been alone since she had moved into the overseer's house after her mother fell ill, excepting the occasional visit from Mr. Levallois. Emily had taken to solitude and self-sufficiency, such as it was, and was starting to become accustomed to it. While she liked the idea of company from time to time, Mr. Levallois bringing her cut white roses, or watching Rawls tending to her chores while she sat alone in the parlor, another part of her considered it an intrusion into the world she had been building for herself.

"Well, you must go do as he says," said Emily. When Rawls had the cart nearly out of sight he turned back toward the overseer's house and saw that Emily remained fixed to the same spot at the edge of the drive, watching yet. Her stillness gave him a chill, and he recalled her old game when they were younger. Standing on a fence post while the birder circled below. The younger Emily laughing and shouting out commands. Rawls feeling like danger had no boundary. She was aloof and distant now. And while he had never thought of Emily's presence as something to celebrate, he now found the depth of the girl's recession into herself even more alarming. Rawls did not think she'd ever play that old game again, but he had started to worry that one far worse might take its place. He pressed the soles of his moccasins firmly on the floorboard of the cart. For a while he'd felt a kind of equilibrium. Not safety, not that at all, but that perhaps he'd found himself at the still center of a storm swirling beyond the boundaries of Beauvais. The look on the girl's face made him wonder. What kind of fence post might she make him stand on soon?

By day's end he and the other men had pulled off the clapboard of the Reids' house. In the evening they went at the barn and the mule stable for the good cedar. By the fifth day they had everything stripped to the foundation. Rawls had fixed up a buyer for most of the scrap, and Levallois let him set aside 10 percent of what he got for it, and he got a good price. Rainy-day money, Levallois called it, though Rawls didn't think much of Confederate dollars. As the sun set and the sky dropped kind of pinkly over top of them, he surveyed the week's work. "Like it was never there, Rawls," Levallois had said. Something about not wanting someone else's history to intrude on his future. "What you think, boys?" he asked his crew. They nodded, though none of them understood why a man would pay to have a perfectly good house torn down and sold off for scrap. White folk's crazy, some of them surely thought. They even put down seed to cover the erased house's footprint. Nothing could be done about the pebblestone road, however, so the road led to nowhere. To an empty meadow in the pinewoods and a circle around a sycamore.

Nurse gave birth to George in an amputation tent at Chimborazo Hospital on the second day of April 1863. She had been doubled over in pain since the previous evening, and the surgeons left her moaning on the blood-soaked floor while they went about their work. The grind of saw on bone. A probe, a finger, or a pair of tongs digging for a minié ball in the flesh of a young man's arm or leg that lay torn open like the entrance to a mine. The firm but quiet voices as the doctors and assistants gave instructions and replies. A limb tossed to the wooden floor with a thump and a small spatter of blood. And Nurse, in the corner of the tent, ignored while she writhed back and forth in pain in ever-decreasing intervals like a wounded metronome.

But late at night the surgeons left, and some of the other nurses came to her as the contractions became a steady, searing pain. The noises of the wounded and delimbed had returned already, the ether and the chloroform having worn off long before, and George entered the world to a chorus of anguished voices, in a room lit by a single sputtering candle that sent its light weakly toward the canvas walls. And in that room Nurse quietly wept, and the bawling child she tightly held added his new voice to the chorus as the sun breached the treetops to the east.

An enlisted man from the quartermaster's office came to see her that afternoon. "Can't take care of no babies here," he said. "Got a message out to your master to collect you both."

Bob Reid heard the news of the child's birth and made his slow mechanical way into the slave quarters not long after Nurse returned to her tent. Those he passed on his way to her either stopped and stared in shock or turned away out of habit. A woman beat a cloth on a washboard in front of Nurse's small tent, which she shared with six others. "Nurse about?" Bob asked.

The woman kept at her washing. "She's inside," she said.

"Is it decent for a man in there?" he asked.

She shrugged. "Just her and the little one."

Bob reached for the flap of the tent and paused before

opening it. He looked at the woman and she waited for whatever it was he seemed about to say. But he only looked at her for a moment longer, pulled the tent open, and went inside. Nurse slept with the baby in her arms, but the child was awake, his eyes moving across the dimness of the tent and pausing at the shadow Bob made in the doorway's light. Bob sat on a cot next to hers, laid his crutch across his knees, and looked at the newborn. Nurse woke and looked at him and clutched her child tighter to her.

"What'll happen to you?" asked Bob.

"Going to master's," she answered.

"Where's that?"

"Beauvais."

"Hmm," Bob grumbled. "That right?"

"It is."

"He's a queer one, that Levallois."

"I can't say, Mr. Reid."

"He's a queer one, I say. You don't need to say."

Nurse regarded him carefully. The baby dozed now in her arms. "You'll be nearby, won't you, Mr. Reid?" she asked.

"I will. My place is very near to it. My daughter has been at Beauvais while I recovered."

"I expect you'll be back about your business soon, Mr. Reid."

"Don't humor me, Nurse. I'm as useless as tits on a bull." He thought of the boy with the broken glasses, the butt of the weapon coming down hard on that poor Pennsylvanian's skull. "If it weren't for my Emily, I'd have liked to died right in that meadow. Shit," he said. "I ain't much better than a nigger now."

Nurse remained quiet.

"You hold on to that little one, Nurse," he said. He did not tell her that his daughter's letters had stopped coming. He did not say that the last one had arrived late in January and was composed of a few formalities and the following lines:

Mother passed last night. She will be buried in the yard near the sycamore tree when there is a warm stretch. Rawls says the ground is too hard right now to dig a proper grave for her. Aurelia died a month ago. She was kept in the root cellar for a while but I don't know what has been done with her. Mr. Levallois is a great comfort to me.

A week after the hospital quartermaster notified Levallois that his contract had been canceled, Rawls readied a carriage to retrieve some property from Chimborazo for his master. Levallois had taken much more interest than normal in Rawls's preparations that morning. For a full hour of the receding darkness, Levallois watched him prepare the rig and the mules for the journey. He waved at Rawls as the carriage rolled off down the drive and toward the city through the coming eastern light. Midmorning Rawls stopped to rest on the high south bank of the James. He listened for the sounds of the ten thousand Federal prisoners on Belle Isle but heard nothing except the wind coursing over the water and its gray-green splash against the stone piers of the railroad bridge. Around noon he crossed over the James, entering the city proper, and he hung his head as he traveled north up Wall and past the hell of Lumpkin's Jail. Rawls steered the rig east again at Broad Street, and slowly the mules dragged the cart over the cobbles and up the steep hill. When he passed over the rickety wooden bridge that spanned the ravine called Bloody Run, the once-green field at the top of Chimborazo Hill sprawled out before him as if it had been occupied by a blaze of white. The low wards of whitewashed wood stretched to the slope of the hill until they seemed to extend to the edge of the world. Tents, too, ringed the acreage, and the blue sky above the camp was veined with cook smoke and plumes of dust roused from the beaten paths between the rows into which the hospital had been arranged. Rawls found the scope of the grounds nearly unbelievable. More people were gathered there on the easternmost of Richmond's seven hills than he had ever seen at one time in his life. Nurses and orderlies darted in and out of tents, their smocks stained with blood as brown as tilled bottomland dirt. The green grass that had previously been the sole occupant of the hilltop had long since been trampled into memory. The dust rose up in swirls again in the warming air, and the white of the scrubbed tents in the bright clear noon stayed with him when he looked away as if he had stared too long at the sun.

He handed a message to the gate guard, still bound with Levallois's seal. He did not know what was written there, only that he was to return to Beauvais promptly with his master's property. Rawls waited at the edge of the hospital for a while. Then, as if in a dream, he saw Nurse walking toward him. He had been leaning against the carriage, and when he saw her he slumped down until he was very nearly sitting in the dirt. He felt as though his breath would flood out of his body entirely, the way water from a spring will tumble out of the earth, clear and fragile as glass. He let his breath out and with it tears streamed over his high cheekbones. He pulled his hat from his head and allowed the tears to proceed soundlessly and without interruption. He caught his breath again, slowly and deliberately, and stood up. He returned his hat to his head as she approached. She carried an infant swaddled in her arm. Nurse's dark face against the background of the hospital remained buried in shadow, and Rawls felt as though an essential part of him was being returned, as dear to him as if his own shadow had come back after being severed for so long. He had not seen her in more than two years. Before the war started. Before Reid sold him and his mother to Levallois. Before his mother joined Reid's wife in fever and death. Rawls recalled Levallois waving as he left that morning, though he did not linger on the thought. His hope that a day like this might come had carried him a great distance, but in the midst of his present joy a very small part of him did wonder if a hope come to fruition would have the strength to carry him farther or if it would now be exhausted.

Beside Nurse walked a white man thin as a switch, iron and leather fixed to his leg and the right sleeve of his coat pinned at the shoulder. Rawls noticed Nurse's hand at the man's elbow. The gentle pressure applied in such a way as to let the man feel his balance might someday return naturally, that her help was useful, but not necessary. "Let them have their pride for now," she would tell him later. "Soon enough it will be gone as well."

The man whom Nurse led toward the carriage resembled Rawls's former owner only a little. The sleeve pinned up at his right shoulder flapped in the breeze. His legs moved stiffly. They reminded Rawls of a scythe without a cutting blade swinging above the dirt.

"Take a good long gander, Rawls," said Reid. "I don't want to feel you staring at my back every time I turn around."

"Pardon, Mr. Reid. It's just been so long since I seen you."

"I take it you missed me, then?" he asked.

"Let me help you up, sir."

Reid swatted away Rawls's outstretched hand as Nurse helped him climb into the rearward-facing backseat of the carriage. "The girl's the one who helps me," he said. "What do you know about my needs?"

Nurse joined Rawls on the driver's bench. He looked at the child without judgment. They knew their true reunion would have to wait, so they began a silent one at the front of the carriage, and Nurse, too, felt her breath push against the walls of her chest, and the tears fell from her unblinking eyes and down her cheeks, until she tasted their sweetness at the corners of her silent mouth. She was overcome with joy, but also dread, for she had known as soon as she saw Rawls slumping down next to the carriage that this reunion had been arranged for reasons she did not understand by the man they would all soon see.

"Take me home, Rawls," said Reid.

Rawls looked at Nurse as if to tell her something, but only turned his head toward the reins again and whipped the mules to get them going.

They retraced Rawls's earlier journey on their return, over the old stone piers of the bridge that spanned the fall line, then climbed the crest of the low river valley where the turnpike began its dusty lurch toward the Piedmont and the endless wave of blue-gray mountains that lay beyond the hills. They almost immediately passed the abandoned terminus of the narrow-gauge line from which Bob and his mule team had derived a living. The wood of the platform was mostly stripped off; some to make lean-tos and hovels along the riverbank that housed the war's destitute and bereft, still more removed to build earthworks and fortifications out toward the wide, flat water of City Point.

Bob knew very little of what had transpired since he'd left with the Volunteer Dragoons at the war's outset. He knew that his wife was dead. That his daughter had been ensconced in the overseer's house at Beauvais Plantation for more than half a year. But he did not know that the house his first slave had built by hand years before her birth had been torn down and scattered among the tinkers and scrappers who picked the land clean of any precious thing like they were opossums after carrion.

He saw the end of the narrow-gauge line and the stripped bones of the warehouse as they passed and said nothing. What am I now? he wondered. To Rawls, no longer a master. To Virginia, no more useful than all the dead men in their graves. And it was what he saw in the eyes of others that vexed him most, for what he saw was their collective shame at his return, at his mere endurance. Not that it would ever be said out loud, he understood very well, but no one is waiting to praise a man whose body is marked up by his failures, especially if his brokenness serves to mark theirs just as well.

They passed the pebble road that stood at the entrance to his land and drove on. "Home, I said, Rawls."

"Mr. Levallois wants me to come to Beauvais first," he said. "You know I got to do what he says now, Mr. Reid," said Rawls.

Rawls steered the carriage down the big house's long drive, flanked on either side by rows of gnarled cedars. Nurse saw Levallois standing at the high point of the front acreage next to a man in a dusty black suit, and she grabbed at Rawls's right knee instinctively. She grabbed it so hard that she hurt him, and at the same time she squeezed George to her side so tightly that he began to bawl. She let go quickly and did not look over at Rawls even when she felt his eyes on her. She sang to the baby softly, and it was hard to hear the words she sang as the newborn boy cried. Nurse looked back at Reid, but his eyes remained fixed to the road down which they'd come, seemingly indifferent to the con-tinuing existence of the world.

"Here they are, sir," Rawls said to Levallois when they pulled abreast of him.

"Good man, Rawls. Good man. Excuse me for a moment while I welcome the return of our conquering hero," Levallois said, then put his foot on the carriage's step. He moved to grab Bob's shoulder but grabbed instead the empty, pinned-up gray fabric of the sleeve. Reid looked at Levallois for a moment with his top teeth bared like a whipped dog and then collected himself. Levallois pulled his hand back and laughed apologetically, then placed the back of his hand softly against the unkempt beard on Reid's cheek, as though he were a sick child. "You've been missed, Bob. Sorely missed. But now you're home and great things are soon to come to pass for both of us."

"I just want to see Emily," he said.

"She's been waiting for you."

Levallois then reached out for Nurse as if to take the baby from her, but she leaned away imperceptibly, leaving him to say, "I bet he'll grow up to be a big strong nigger, Nurse. What do you think, Rawls?"

Rawls stared at the backs of the mules. "Yes, sir," he said quietly. "I expect you're right."

Levallois leaned in toward Rawls and almost whispered, "He hardly even looks like a pickaninny, does he, Rawls? I tell you, the child looks damn near like an Indian, his skin's so light, don't you think?"

Bob was lost in thought, wondering what world he had returned to. He'd dreamed a million dreams in the fever of late summer, and on into last winter when the light fell meagerly from the sky as though measured out in dirty cupfuls. "Where is she?" he asked. "Did she get looked after?"

Levallois sighed. "I must admit I felt it necessary to step in. The first time I sent Rawls to look in on her she was a week away from eating the leather off her shoes, God help her." He took his foot off the step and put his hands in his pockets. "Your troubles are now over, Bob."

Nurse and Rawls listened to the conversation with their chins against their chests as though a certain posture was as good as deafness in the white men's eyes. George was quiet again, asleep in her arms. If the world was a different place, she would have shaken her head and said how none of it was true, that the girl didn't have no trouble that the Frenchman wouldn't add on to quick and heavy enough to knock her on her narrow behind from the weight of it all. She won't be getting up from that. But Nurse knew she was in the beating heart of Virginia and not that other world, not the one she had begun to go to in her mind, the place where she'd been told a million islands hid themselves above the black water of the Dismal Swamp, and free people lived on them beneath the tupelo cypresses and high white cedars. And in Virginia the truth had not mattered for a long time and would not matter for a good long while yet. The only thing that matters here, she thought, is what people are willing to believe. Lots of dead black folks would attest to that if they were still around to do it. There ain't no telling the kinds of madness people will believe, but the truth never seemed to Nurse to stand a chance.

Bob, too, was unconvinced by Levallois's earnestness. Troubles don't end, he thought. It sounded more like Levallois was reading to him from Reid's own eulogy. He's got my old boy toting me around like one of his empty hogsheads. Bob thought of the boy who rifled his pockets at Mechanicsville again. Him putting on the Pennsylvanian's smashed glasses with a smile like he got them for Christmas. The little dance he danced afterward.

"In a way," he said, "I've felt like a father to her in your absence."

"Is that a fact?" asked Bob.

"And now," Levallois went on, choosing his words carefully, "I see that my feelings were misguided in that respect. I no longer see her as a daughter, but rather as a bride."

Bob instinctively tensed to take on a threatening posture, but the effect produced was only a loud creaking sound from his leg brace and the gray sleeve flapping impotently in the breeze blowing over the windy hill.

"Bob, I've thought often about getting word to you so I might properly ask for her hand. But you must trust me. This arrangement is the best for all of us."

Bob waved his remaining hand dismissively. "You just fetch my daughter and tell this boy to carry us home. We can talk about the rest of it later."

"I won't hear of it, Bob," said Levallois. "Not with it near dark already. They say there's Federal cavalry about," he said. "Emily's in the overseer's house nearby. Stay with her tonight at least."

"Fine. Yes. Take me to her."

"Good. Good. Rawls," Levallois said, "why don't you and Nurse get Mr. Reid set up." He clapped his hands once, and the sharpness of the sound made Bob jump. Levallois laughed. "It's a reunion," he said. "There is nothing better than a reunion."

Levallois and the minister silently watched the carriage travel down the road between the ornamental cedars until it curved off into open fields and passed behind a stand of old-growth beech trees and disappeared.

"Will we need to adjust the date, Mr. Levallois?" the minister said.

"Reverend, I couldn't put such strain on Mr. Reid, now could I?"

That night Levallois sent Rawls on an errand back to Richmond. A pretense. No moon as the master of Beauvais stalked the dark edge of the road that led to the slave cabins. Nurse looked out and saw the burning ember of his pipe through the warped window glass of the cabin she soon would share with Rawls. But not tonight. Tonight she smelled the bright and burley wafting through the air as a warning. She went to douse the lamp but passed a window as she did. "A favor, Nurse," he said to announce his presence. She opened the door and stood in the doorframe. She saw him leaning against a pine in the darkness. A man as seemingly out of place in darkness as in light. His shirt lay sloppily open beneath his coat. The white skin all that trespassed against midnight's implicit safety. She did not speak.

"I feel like a young man again, Nurse. I feel alive."

"I'm glad to hear it," she said. Each time one of them spoke she tried to close the door a little more without making it obvious.

He knocked his pipe on the tree he had been leaning

against, the ember extinguished. "Won't you invite me in?" he said.

"Where's Rawls?" she asked quietly.

"He's away. Won't be back for some time. Such a dutiful man."

He stepped inside. George slept in a curl of blankets next to Nurse's bed.

Mr. Levallois did not know how unremarkable he was. But Nurse did. For all his cultivated distance and machinations, he was of a type she knew all too well. An insignificant tooth in a gear that would continue turning whether one broke off or not. She had met dozens like him in her life, and could figure the hundreds and thousands that played the same role all throughout the South. He pretended at sophistication, but his next violence was never more than a whim away, or at a distance closed by some minor disappointment. And she could not say for sure if she or Rawls or both would die by his hand, but she figured whoever's hand it was would look enough like his as to make no difference. What counted as a blessing in this world made her want to curse God, to dismiss the notion of him with the ease with which Rawls dismissed life's whole absurd affair. To say, *Today will be a hard day, and tomorrow even harder,* and leave that as sufficient commentary. But now was not the time for *yet.* Now she must deal with *again.* She opened the door. She knew everything he would say and all the ways the hatred of his own flesh would be twisted and forced upon her. He was, like all of them, predictable. Nurse tried to surrender to it, but in the end she struggled just enough to make him eager.

*   *   *

The next morning Bob left his daughter sleeping in the overseer's house. He limped out into the frost-hardened yard and made his way toward the back acreage, shouting for Nurse, but he received no answer and did not have the strength to knock on every cabin door. When he got back to the overseer's house Emily was waiting for him. "Get your things," he said. "We're going home."

"It's not there, Papa," Emily said.

She had seemed a child when he'd left. As he took her in that morning, leaning against the porch railing and pulling a knit shawl around her tall shoulders to guard against the cold, he recognized how much she had changed. She was nearly sixteen now, and there was a part of him that mistook her despondency for a natural element of maturity. For a moment, he assumed she was speaking in metaphor. "I know this has all been hard on you, too, Emily," he said. "I want to make my absence up to you if I can. But we're going away from this place. That man's not like us. I don't want you around him if I can help it, and I'm damn sure gonna try."

"No, Papa. It's not there anymore."

She told her father that after his letters stopped coming, Mr. Levallois suggested he be made executor of her father's estate. The papers were drawn up and signed quickly, in the midst of her grief. He had fed her and given her shelter, and there had been no word from Bob Reid to make her think he would ever return. So she let Mr. Levallois take over, as she believed he would not steer her wrong.

Bob began to say, "We'll petition the courts. They'll see the position you were in...," but his words trailed off as the true nature of his predicament loomed. Levallois could afford an army of lawyers large enough in size to rival the one Bob Reid had just been discharged from. Everything he had ever owned was now a minor portion of a huge portfolio that a man of Bob Reid's station would never be allowed to split. He didn't even have an income, other than a new law passed in Richmond to give out benefits to veterans that he was not prepared to put much faith in. He looked at his daughter and saw that she had been twice deceived. First by him and the Commonwealth, when he abandoned her to go and fight on its behalf. And then by Mr. Levallois, though he did not blame Emily for that. "Help me get the horses. I want to see it."

"Papa," she said again. "There's nothing left to see."

In the warming morning light, he and Emily rode from the overseer's house to their old land. In a year the first iron on Levallois's new railway line to Raleigh would be laid across the same ground Bob and Emily had once called home. As Emily told him how everything had been sold off for scrap, Bob realized that Levallois would never have been able to put the deal together if circumstances had not allowed him to acquire the land as cheaply as he had.

Bob dismounted with his daughter's help. He walked through the emptiness of his land and imagined what it was to become. Metal, gravel, and pitched ties further burying his wife's grave. The outline of his daughter's childhood home still visible as an accidental bed where bluebells and purple phlox thrived among high wild grasses. He stood for a moment in disbelief before saying quietly, "I'll get it back, Emily. I promise. I don't know how, but I will."

Emily looked at her broken father shuffling around the property as though its landmarks were still there, passing instinctively through a space where there had once been a swinging gate. He let himself slump unceremoniously to the ground with his back to her. Emily was humiliated on his behalf. She both loved him and loathed him. His injury and helplessness. And while she did not have the heart to say it to her father, she knew that Mr. Levallois would never give anything back to them but more emptiness.

She was married to Levallois as spring turned to summer. The morning of, Bob Reid looked in his dressing mirror and hardly recognized himself. Nearly a year gone since he'd been wounded at Mechanicsville. On his best days he thought a wagon with a busted axle or a poorly mended stretch of fence could be compared favorably with what was left of him: the leg brace, his empty sleeve, the sum of it all being just another useless and poorly man-made thing.

Emily had assented to the marriage, but she remained impenetrable to Bob. He asked her for strength and had assured her again and again that he knew what he was doing and that this was for the best. *Be strong and trust me,* he would say. Bob Reid knew it was cruel to lean on whatever strength his daughter still had left, but he knew he had none of his own, or only just enough to quiet the voices telling him to take his shotgun to the barn and paint the haystacks with his brains. What had life been like for her in the two years since he'd left? She did not say when asked and he no longer asked. He tried to give her the yellow kepi she'd admired when he first volunteered, but she'd wept at the sight of it. He obsessed over lines in the letters she'd sent before they'd stopped. *Mr. Levallois says…Mr. Levallois says…Mr. Levallois says.* Since his return, they'd passed in the overseer's house like the other was a ghost. A second look to be sure the figure was real, perhaps a shudder and a word to ward it off.

As the wagon stopped in the circle drive before the ceremony began, he reached for his daughter's hand. Emily looked at him. With a pitiful smile to try to hide her growing resentment of him, she said, "It's too late, Papa."

Bob withdrew further into the moody silence Levallois had long since taken for complete capitulation and Emily for further abandonment. He leaned stoically against his brace after they arrived. Levallois waited for his bride where the ancient sycamore still stood. He watched his daughter walk the pebble drive until she stopped across from Levallois and looked timidly toward the preacher. Reid's only desire in the world was to say to her once more, *My daughter, this is for the best. I swear on your mother, if you trust me, I can set this world right.* But Bob Reid did not say those words.

She looked down at the ground as the reverend began to speak. Ever so briefly, with one shattering glance in his direction, Emily told her father her world had ended. She was not wrong. Her world was ended. But she did not even know why she wasn't wrong, didn't know that her description of the end of something that seemed to her unique and personal was equally true and applicable to the state of things beyond her appropriately petulant complaint. The world was ended. Reid knew this. And he loved her for it; that her insouciant rage and disappointment flooded into the void the world had left behind. The bluecoats on horseback already cantered at its edges. The speculators soon would come to make more valuations and assessments. He looked away from her in shame, and lowered his eyes. What kind of man am I, to give her a broken world and turn around and take that from her, too? And there she waited for Levallois to take her hand, telling the truth in the way we all do best, when we are trying to say something else, when we do not even realize it is the truth we mean to tell.

Mr. Levallois requested that the wedding should begin with a reading from the Song of Solomon. And so the preacher slowly interrupted the silence with words about a dark beauty and a neglected vineyard before ending with a reading from Genesis, proclaiming that those who gathered among those pale summer-lit grasses on the hill were just and righteous among their generations, and so, too, would be all those who followed from this marriage. Finally, he pronounced that Emily was now wedded for all eternity in the eyes of God to Mr. Levallois.

She looked at her father again and turned away from the deep shame she saw on his face. Her body tensed and she began to feel an increasing bitterness toward the lies the world had raised her to unquestioningly accept. Did she ever have a choice? It seemed to Emily that her whole life had been mapped out already by the minister's God, or her father and Mr. Levallois, or all the men just like them who insisted the world was exactly as they described. She was beginning to see all the ways that she had been lied to with a new clarity, that they would say anything at all if it made them feel better about themselves. She wondered what it would be like to choose for herself, if it was possible to choose surrender and then claim a secret life that would not be determined by anyone but herself. She watched her father in his great shame, and she was not sure if he even knew that he was living in the lie, too. She was not sure she cared much about the lies other people told themselves anymore. Now she stood alone in summer air so thick it felt like the whole breadth of the sky had been weighed down by an invisible anchor, and she began to feel her fear dissolve. Mr. Levallois was talking to the minister, and her father stood apart from all in his scarcely hidden shame. She would live her own life now. Whatever it looked like to the outside world, whatever circumstances might make up her surroundings, she resolved that she would be the single master of her mind and heart. And she barred the doors to both forever.

They spent their wedding night in a doomed hotel in Richmond, a city profoundly in denial of the fact that its inevitable ruin had already begun. The sounds of a bread riot a mere three blocks from their room grew steadily louder throughout the evening. "Close the window, please, Mr. Levallois," she said. There was a knock at their door. Two black men in white coats and gloves served them dinner in their suite, silently attending to their needs in a performance so exquisitely executed that their subservience and decorous manners seemed completely natural to almost every guest who encountered them.

Levallois smiled, said, "Of course, dear one," and shut it, flipping the latch closed with a metallic click.

He took the three steps toward the fireplace and put his hand on her shoulder. She flinched ever so slightly, but then regained her composure so quickly that only someone who expected it to happen would have perceived the loss of it. Her anxiety angered him. He had hoped that on this night there would be a different manner of concession. He had taken his liberties often enough over the years. But now he had a wife, *she* was his wife, and he expected her to respond with something like passion or desire. No. Her body responded to his touch in the same unmistakable pattern: a tense resistance followed by a kind of recognition, finally giving way to a dull, meaningless surrender.

Emily had been to Richmond only twice in her life. She found the endless stone and brick suffocating. In a storm she would have heard the water rushing past the piers that held up the nearby railway bridge. But there was no storm. The night was clear and humid and smelled like smoke and sewage and penned horses even though their room was high above the level of the street. She turned to look out the window. The occasional spire above the monotonous brick. A smokestack puffing in the moonlit night. She had been happy once, she thought, before circumstance took her from her solitude and brought her to Levallois. She would be happy only, she decided, if she were ever able to find that solitude again.

They ate their cold dinner in silence. Levallois built a fire in the fireplace in spite of the warm and humid evening so he would have something to look at other than his young wife. She went into the adjoining room and tried to will herself to do what must be done. It could be said that Levallois began to love her that night precisely because she was further than ever from being one of his possessions. But this did not make her love him back.

She came out of the room naked. Her gray eyes were illuminated by the firelight, two clouds passing before the moon. "Put out the lamp," Emily asked. "Please." She was not afraid of him anymore. And while she did not know what to expect, she told herself she was making a choice. Better the devil you know, they say. His suffocating weight troubled her most, not the pain, and time moved indifferently forward; then and now, here and there, leveling possibility. She shut her eyes and tried to lose herself in the emptiness she felt, but the thought of endless nights and days like this remained. Eventually, she stopped caring whether the lamp was lit at night or not.

EIGHT

MERE WEEKS AFTER Lottie Bride's strange encounter with the amiable old Virginian, she met a man named Charlie Prentis, who would be her husband for the eighteen months prior to her reaching her majority. He drove truck for an outfit called Tar River Freight and had come into the diner a quarter through a long-haul route to Mobile, Alabama, and halfway through a case of Schlitz. They danced in the parking lot at 4:00 a.m., and the emptiness of the mercury-vapor lights at the nearby intersection made them look like ghosts to the drivers of the few cars that passed them by.

Charlie had been, above all else, an inveterate hypocrite. The same man who after making love with her in the cab of his '50 Kenworth said, "Goddamn, girl, your mind is on fire. I never seen anything like it," would also say, when a little further into a case of Schlitz, that she was a no-good half-coon bitch, that there weren't no such people as the Croatan, and that he couldn't wait to get out of that back-water and on the road again. The marriage was mercifully brief, ending when Charlie drove his rig straight through a sharp curve above the New River in West Virginia and drowned. His body was not discovered until nearly two weeks later when it was spotted by an executive of the Chesapeake and Ohio Railroad while waiting for his family to arrive for their vacation. In what would have been considered a very strange coincidence, if not an augury, had it been known by anyone, the shade of purple Charlie's skin had turned over his ten days in the water was indistinguishable from the color of the bruises he'd left on Lottie's face the morning he fired up his diesel engine for the last time and drove it toward his death.

By 1965 she had settled comfortably in a small cottage of three rooms at the end of Pocahontas Avenue in Deltaville, Virginia. She lived alone and would do so for many more years, her brief marriage in her teens having disabused her of the idea that her solitude reflected poorly on her rather than on the world she decided to leave behind after her husband's death. At twenty-five she took a fill-in job with the post office that landed her in that small Virginia town right out on the edge of America, and her mail route carried her over back roads stitched intricately into the endless coastal woods through which, from time to time, she'd catch a glimpse of the great bay as it unfolded toward the ocean.

Most of her free time was spent either on her porch, looking out over the gray granite riprap and green water of the Chesapeake, or in her garage, which she'd found to be a more than adequate studio for her art. She worked mainly in oils, reproducing the South that she drove through each day with an amateur's honesty and a native's stubborn affection for all its peculiarities and contradictions. Here a black streak on canvas stood in the wide water's stead, there a dotting of bright color on a gray rectangle looked like the small bands of beach along the bay in summer's bright light. Many people in Deltaville and its environs had one of Lottie's pictures hanging in their houses, but few of them felt that they knew her, though with a wave from the window of her jeep, Lottie often left people with the idea that whoever did was fortunate indeed. A long time passed in this way. Many years, in fact. She moved from youth into adulthood, and from adulthood into what should have been the middle of her life. *It's not a bad life, after all,* Lottie would have said if asked. Though she was alone, she was very rarely lonely, and Lottie Bride was more or less contented with the order of her days.

But by the time autumn arrived in Deltaville, Virginia, in 1984, Lottie felt that something was wrong. She thought of the old Virginian more now than she had in the nearly thirty years since those brief hours she'd spent with him so many Junes before in North Carolina. The previous summer she'd met a man named Billy Rivers who owned an all-in-one store in Saluda, where one minor highway splits off from another and heads eastward toward the bay and Deltaville. He sold bait and tackle, a few secondhand guns, cold beer in the working half of a cooler and warm beer in the broke half. He would sometimes fix a busted motor or sagging shocks in the parking lot out back. He was unremarkable, about thirty-five years old, not really good or bad looking;

the kind of man you might not notice unless he spoke to you and would still have a hard time describing afterward no matter how long the conversation went. He had a mustache he kept neatly trimmed and a potbelly and was going bald, but he covered his baldness with a blue-and-white Mopar hat, which struck a lot of folks down there as an affectation, though a curious one, as he drove a perfectly maintained Ford F-100, brown in color, with a long bed and a white camper shell.

She went on a few dates with him after he'd fixed an old beater she'd accepted as payment for a series of paintings for a friend. Lottie thought he was timid and uninteresting at first, but on the third date she realized that he was neither timid nor uninteresting, but in fact was simply listening to her with complete attention, that he found her fascinating and beautiful, and that he seemed content to allow her a glimpse into the life they might share, one in which she could feel the ease and comfort of solitude even when he was with her, only asking that he receive the same feeling back in kind. She knew he had a young son he would not talk about; an ex-wife he was not allowed to see. She also knew that he was kind and gentle and that both of these qualities were anchored to an implacable despair around which his whole being seemed to orbit.

A few years before he met Lottie, Billy had put the bottle down for good. He had decided to live the way that other people lived, or to at least transform his life into the best approximation of the lives of others he was capable of. This made him a better man in many ways. But it is true that he was a worse man for it, too, in other, less obvious ways, because in his mind his whole life now blossomed from dishonest roots. His wife, Amy, left him. She took back her maiden name, Bartle, and gave it to their son instead of his. She'd become pregnant during one of their last good patches, both of them thinking that by bringing something new into the world they might recover some old thing they had lost. It did not work. She took their son, John, to live in a little rented house on the other side of the James outside of Richmond, an hour-and-a-half drive from the house they'd bought as newlyweds when he left the army in 1971. He thought that if he changed, his wife might stay, but that is not what happened. His changing only made his past transgressions all the more intolerable to his wife, and so she filed a writ against him. When Billy read what she had sworn before the court, he saw nothing he was not guilty of. And even though he and his wife both knew he would not do those things again, he also readily accepted that that fact was not enough to save their marriage. So he made no argument against the writ, and let her escape his orbit the way he supposed a good man would.

But there was some quality in Billy Rivers beyond what remained unpardonable that Lottie grew to count on by the time the weather turned colder. He had moved his things from the cabin he kept on the Piankatank River to her little house on Pocahontas Avenue only a month after they first met. He was a shy but enthusiastic lover, and when they were finished he would carefully take off his square-framed glasses, fold them up, and place them on the nightstand in an orderly manner, just in front of his wallet. This was all part of Billy's curiously meticulous nature, common to a lot of ex-drunks, who often keep their constant fear of impending doom when they go on the wagon but add to it a belief that this same doom can be warded off if they arrange their lives just so. He told her he had worn the same pair of glasses since the army had issued them to him in 1968, before which time he had not known there was anything wrong with his eyes. Lottie thought there was a lot to be said for a man who looked after such small things so well, things that most of us treat with indifference and spend a lifetime discarding, and so she forgave him some for his failure to give the truly important things in his life the same attention.

Lottie did not ask him about Vietnam, though she knew he had been there for two years when he was nineteen and twenty years old. And he did not have much to say about it, except at night, when he would yelp and holler in his sleep. It got to be where Lottie could hardly sleep herself unless his fit had come and gone. Billy's song, his little lullaby, she called it privately. After a while she began to depend on that as well. She did not say anything to him about his terrors, though she would hold him tightly to her when they came, and sometimes he would wake up after, with Lottie holding him as though she were herself adrift in some terrible storm. She did not say anything to him because she was sure he would tell her the truth if she asked, would tell her anything and everything about his life without a moment's hesitation. Lottie felt unusually comforted by this certainty, that if the truth is always close at hand it does not need to be said.

Billy had only been as honest as he was with Lottie one other time in his life. When he was twenty-seven years old he drove to the McGuire Veterans Hospital south of Richmond and asked to see a psychiatrist. He hoped that by driving out to Richmond he would preserve some notion of the safety we very often seek in anonymity. They exchanged small talk, and when the doctor asked him how much he was drinking, Billy cut the figure in half, thinking they could then move on from the subject. He was surprised when the doctor told him twelve beers every day meant he was probably alcoholic. The terrors of the night had not come yet. Billy drowned his ghosts back then. But the terrors of the day were ever present. He told the doctor that sometimes, with a sideways glance in a mirror or out of the corner of his eye, he would see a child burned so badly that its skin came off in black coils, like a snake's, he said. Or that he very often smelled the burning of man-made things, of people, of villages. And he also said that he felt like he had not killed enough of them gook fuckers, or not the right ones anyway, and what the hell was he supposed to do about that? The doctor asked him if the hatred in him made him afraid. "I don't hate anyone. I don't feel anything at all," Billy replied. "That's what scares me."

"And why does that scare you?"

He didn't answer. *A man who can't hate can't love* is what he wanted to say, thinking of his young wife, Amy, how he knew she deserved better than what he could give her, and that he did not think he was capable of giving her anything but far too large a share of his pain.

"How long is it gonna be like this?" he asked instead.

"How long is it gonna be like what, Billy? Talk to me."

"This," he said. "You know. All this bullshit."

"Oh," the doctor answered. He leaned forward, crossing his legs and putting both elbows on his knee, his hands tucked up under his chin. "Forever, Billy. It's gonna be like this forever."

He felt a little better when he left, though that wasn't saying much.

Lottie and Billy got looks sometimes when they went inland, to Tappahannock or to Richmond. It wasn't much of an issue farther out on the bay, because according to Billy watermen divide the world up differently than other people, into watermen and everyone else. Other divisions have to be learned. And anyway, even in Tappahannock or Richmond, most folks would decide she must be Mattaponi or something after a few minutes, even if to them she might look like a light-skinned black girl at first, a nigger in the woodpile, at least, they'd tell themselves, and then they'd let them be. Lottie was forty-three years old when she met Billy, ten years older than he was. And she had learned things by then that Billy didn't know, would perhaps never really know, one of which was that people were going to make decisions about them without any input from either Lottie or Billy, as people generally don't want your own ideas about your life clouding their thinking when they are making up their mind about you.

The weather was remarkably warm a few days after Christmas that year. They had a routine by then, which the sunshine and a high of nearly eighty degrees happily up-ended. Lottie would work most of her days off in her garage studio, and Billy would get into his immaculate truck in the morning before she woke and drive out to the shop in Saluda, where he'd spend a few hours making small talk and occasionally a few sales. At around three in the afternoon he'd drive back to the little house on Pocahontas Avenue, make sandwiches and coffee, and wait for Lottie to take a break and join him. They had two tattered nylon folding chairs set up above the riprap for when it was nice, and Lottie would laugh until she wept when Billy would say, casually and without self-consciousness, "Let's dine alfresco, then," because sometimes the funniest thing in the world to her was Billy putting on airs, which he did not do often, and anyway did only because he loved her more than he would have thought possible when she laughed and he did not mind at all if she sometimes laughed at him.

If it was cool or cold they would sit on the screened-in porch on Adirondack chairs that Billy had made, with a little kerosene heater going between the chairs. Lottie had begun a new work at the end of summer. She did not say anything to Billy about the specifics of her art and he did not ask about it other than "How's it going, darling?" Whatever she replied, he always seemed to know the right thing to say. If she was frustrated he would encourage her; if she was excited, he would say very simply, "Good. That's real good." Billy did not know or care very much about art, but she didn't need or want him to say anything else because he knew she had real talent. He knew this about her because he had heard her say it once, though she said it in a manner that had no relationship to arrogance, only as a fact she wanted to convince herself of, one that slips away too easily if left unmentioned, the way one might say, below the breath, *Thirty days hath September.* So he had no reason to doubt her, because in all the time they had together there were no lies told in the house on Pocahontas Avenue.

The night before that warm day in December Billy sang his song again. When he woke, Lottie was clinging to him tightly. He had a vague memory of fear, but he forgot it as soon as he felt her body pressed tightly against him. The sheets were still wet with his sweat. He was embarrassed for a moment. He had pissed the bed when he was drunk sometimes, but then he remembered he did not have to do that anymore, or be embarrassed that he used to do it, because he would tell Lottie about that, too, if that was what she wanted to know about him. The morning was already warm. Neither of them minded the dampness much.

Lottie said, "You all right, Billy?"

By way of answering he turned toward her and held her, too, until the force of their holding each other reached an equilibrium so effortless they felt their purpose on earth was to stay that way forever. She decided she liked his potbelly quite a bit and giggled. "What?" he said. And so she told him and he smiled. They made love all day and when the sun started going down behind them they went outside and jumped into the great green waters of the Chesapeake.

The water was frigid, though the air was warm. They were naked and as free as two people had ever been. They loved each other completely, though they did not bother to say so. It seemed unnecessary to say a thing so undeniable. When they ran their hands through the water, it lit up with a blue-green glow, and their bodies lit up when the water ran down their skin. That night they swam in winter stars.

By the time the New Year came, Lottie was finished with her newest painting. They stayed at the Jefferson Hotel in Richmond to celebrate. He got down on one knee at the top of the grand staircase. Lottie laughed and Billy was glad. By February they were married in the little clapboard chapel out by Stingray Point. They had no guests and they did not find the ceremony diminished for it. By March she was dying.

NINE

ALL BUT THE most desperate cases knew the war was over before it actually ended. After Gettysburg in July of '63, sons from battlefields all over the South began to come home. At first it was in twos and threes spread out over days and weeks and months. And finally in those last days of the war their numbers grew until hardly a cold day at the end of '64 went by when they wouldn't be seen in a solitary retreat to the safety of their homes, or in some ragtag band surrendered to some new version of their former lives. Some came on foot, the top of a hat cresting a gray winter hill in the distance. Others came on the back of horse-drawn carts that spent the preceding days depositing their cargo at unnamed crossings, in front of the white chipped-paint walls of modest country churches, and, in a few cases, in places unmarked by human habitation. But that they came was undeniable, and the fact Bobby Lee still waved the Stars and Bars did not provide the same hope it once did. John Talbot made his way toward what home he had as well, but slowly. The war was surely over. His work was not.

In early 1865 two weeks of rain pelted the earth between the James and Appomattox Rivers. Clouds the color of an old iron hammer hung so low in the sky he sometimes had to fight the urge to reach up and keep them from swinging down on him. He followed the sounds of battle as they traveled west, and he stopped in the aftermath of muddy fields to pick up what he could of value. For four years he'd sold watches, rings, and metal buttons to pawnbrokers from Petersburg to Winchester. He collected gold fillings from the teeth of still-stiff corpses. Shoes he sold to passing armies or traded them to runaways with bare and bloodied feet for the last precious things they could carry in their flight. After the Siege of Petersburg the previous summer, he took a cartful of bones he'd dug out of the crater to a Fredericksburg fertilizer manufacturer. The pile was so tall it seemed to John to cast a hundred-yard shadow beneath the August sun. "These is horse bones only, right, young feller?" the payment man had said. And John replied that he believed horses was what they had been once but now they was bones and bones was bones and did he want them or not?

He kept a collection of tintypes and letters that he could not read in a pack he'd taken off a Yankee at Cold Harbor. Sometimes at night he would hold the pictures up to firelight and look for a resemblance to Spanish Jim, but he did not find him or anyone who favored him and he did not know what he would have done even if he did. The dog that kept him warm throughout those long nights after Spanish Jim was killed by that dark-haired man still followed him.

She did not have a name anymore, though sometimes he would try out different ones to see if she would help him recall what her name had been when she sat at the edge of the river and watched him put the smooth round river stones he'd used to weight old Spanish Jim's pockets so he would stay underneath the water at the ferry landing. Now she would disappear for a week, sometimes even two, and then he would see her emerge from a wild meadow at the edge of a country road a quarter mile out ahead of him, the stump of her tail wagging enthusiastically, her face the very picture of assured indifference.

She rode with him when they crossed the swollen Appomattox on an abandoned pontoon bridge in March, her front paws sprawled out over the buckboard next to his feet. He did not think he had ever been this far south. He covered the dog with a spare waxed coat. He caught up with the destruction not long after crossing the Appomattox River, brown and formless in its rain-swelled width. He held back until the battle passed farther west, until the dead were still and the living marched off toward a different death and he could go about his scavenging in peace.

A break in the weather. The sky gray with the memory of winter rains now passed. Songbirds darted among the pines. He tried to hit a squirrel with a rock to share something to eat with the dog, but he could not hit one. They chattered and squawked. Does and fawns bounded between the plumb-straight trees, and the dog sometimes bounded after them when she was bored and would return in inevitable shame to whimper at his feet.

171

He woke to sunlight falling through needles. The ground damp and firm. The dog gone already in the early morning. He listened for the sounds of fighting but heard nothing. Fog rose up from the field beyond his hideout in the trees, and he put on his shoes and dressed and walked into the first warm air he could recall for many months. He looked down the road to the west and did not see movement, only the stillness and quiet of a Virginia spring day that the scavenged items on his cart would fill with the music of their shifting to and fro. He turned back to ready the cart. His mule's ears twitched side to side as she ate the hay he'd set out for her and then pitched forward as a voice called out.

"What you doing out here?"

John turned around and saw a boy about his age wearing a Confederate uniform. The coat was open to a red gingham shirt that was also open to his bare smooth chest and he wore no hat over his blond curls. Round-lensed glasses perched atop his nose. As the boy approached, John could see a star-shaped crack in one of the lenses. "I'm fixing to move along here is all," he said.

"What outfit you with?"

John continued getting the mule and the cart ready to travel. They were all the way out in the road. "I ain't with no outfit. I'm just going down the road."

The boy came closer. He had a pistol on his right hip. A big curved knife dangled comfortably next to his leg in a loose grip in his left hand, as though he never found the need to sheathe it. "War's been going a long time not to have picked no side yet," the boy said.

"They come signed me up a while back, but they sent me on after a couple weeks. Said I didn't have no head for soldiery."

John, being somewhat immune to fear by disposition, was content to answer the boy's questions as honestly as he knew how. This is not to say he was inclined to courage, more that he was unable to wrap his mind around the particulars of any given human interaction. So as he talked he looked the boy in the eyes and fixated on the cracked lenses of his glasses that sometimes appeared in the refracted sunlight like an earthbound star and sometimes seemed to take on the shape of a rose on account of a red spatter that had collected in the lenses' fine fractures.

"Why you giving me that look?" the boy asked.

"We talking is all," answered John. "It ain't no special look. It's a talking look like folks told me I ought to."

The boy rubbed the tip of the blade up and down his pant leg as though scratching an itch. "Naw. That's a look like you think I owe you something."

"We ain't never had no business. It ain't whatever kind of look you thinking."

"I'll tell you what," the boy said with disgust. "You better stop with that Yankee eyeballing, acting like I ain't done what's required of me. You as bad as these goddamn coons looking at me like a freeman would, like I owe somebody something."

John went back to rigging up the cart. Over his shoulder he said, "I'm gonna be on my way." He felt the blade press into the skin on the back of his neck. He then felt the boy put more weight behind it. The wound burned as surely as if the boy had put a match to it. A warm trickle of blood ran down between his shoulder blades and he felt the boy's breath hot in his ear.

"You ain't leaving yet, goddamn it!"

The dog barked her deep throaty bark to his left. John felt the knife come off his neck. The quick swishing sound of leather relieved of metal followed by a bang and flash turned his dull mind into an equilibrium of high-pitched sound. The blood ran down the back of his neck and over his shoulders in narrow runnels where it dripped down his chest. He turned around and saw the boy mouthing at him angrily, but he could not hear anything except for that one unearthly note filling the entirety of his being. The boy pointed the pistol at him, but John looked all around him for the source of the sound. He saw the dog lying dead in front of the cart. It seemed she had lunged at the boy and took a ball in her lower jaw, which was missing now, and her tongue lolled down in the bloody dirt of the road where her jaw should have been. John looked up at the sky, and at first he thought the sound might be coming from the east, but then it seemed to come from the west and south and north and even up under his feet from the center of the earth, which is where someone had once told him hell was.

The boy was still yelling at him when the sounds of the world began to creep into his head again. Telling him to get back where he belonged. To get the hell away from here and go back where he belonged. John did not know where that was. He had no map. He had never slept under a roof in his life, except for the two weeks he spent in the Virginia infantry before they told him he was not fit to be a soldier. He went to the dog and picked her up and put her on the buckboard and covered her disfigured muzzle with her paws. The dog would sometimes lie on him at night and kept him warm and would occasionally lick the dirt from his face when it collected there. He hopped onto the seat and flicked the reins until the mule walked off the way they'd come, away from the boy with the cracked glasses who had cut his neck and shot his dog and screamed himself hoarse about him not owing the world a thing.

John Talbot steered his cart onto the northbound road toward Chesterfield. He wanted the gray-eyed girl to know her dog had not died alone. A low standard, any reasonable person would admit, perhaps ridiculously so, but to do one's best means only that, and to be better than one was requires that we had once been worse. His cart was not empty, but it was nearly so, and after picking up the dog and placing her at his feet, he had no more interest in the things he'd collected from the war's uncountable dead.

He stopped after crossing the Appomattox over the same abandoned pontoon bridge he'd crossed a few days before on his way south. The dog's eyes were queerly open. The left one remained disconcertingly wide, an aperture through which light passed pointlessly, as though the fundamental shock of her death had not occurred in the past but was instead elaborately fixed in an eternal present tense. The right eye, drooping some, appeared to John to flutter in the otherwise pleasant gusts of spring wind, and though perceptiveness was not a strength of his, he was quite sure he felt the fluttering eye whether he looked at it or not. But he no longer had the capacity to acknowledge the pitiful nature of her remaining injuries. Despite the fact that he sometimes still looked down at her while they rode, at the blood speckled in a pattern not dissimilar to the ticking of her coat, by some miracle his mind pardoned him from the greatest punishment of all: comprehension. He went to the back of the cart and looked for something more substantial than the waxed coat to cover her. After some digging, he managed to find a Union blanket underneath a collection of thirteen cavalry sabers he had taken some months before from a battlefield whose name he'd never know. A bright red ribbon was tied around the swords. He wrapped the birder in the blanket and tied the red ribbon in a bow around it. Some poor fool had once used that length of smooth cloth to hold his britches up, until he was killed in a field outside of Petersburg, if John recalled correctly. He put the dog, now bundled in her blanket, back on the buckboard at his feet. He flicked the reins, and they rolled on. Petersburg had been good picking, John might have said on a different day, if he had cause to think about it. But he would not have known *why* to tell it. The simple fact was this: it was hard to find a soul left anywhere on earth who believed that there was dignity in death.

Two days later he passed the mines after crossing over the Chesterfield County line, still at least an hour away from the ferry landing or the road that led to it. He watched the miners emerge from a shaft, one after another, as if crawling out of a hastily dug grave. Most put their hands up to their brows for a few moments after stumbling into the clearing on legs stiff as rusted locks, for even the fast retreat of evening's light was bright enough to blind them, emerging as they had from a dark so total as to make the occasional spark from pick on stone shine as brief and bright as a bolt of lightning. The men, coal dark and blending into the arriving night, kept their candles lit as they stretched and scooped water from pails. The light danced nimbly near the structures, around the hoist and sheave wheel and under the gallows frame. Some of the men began to douse their heads with water, but it was by then too dark to tell if anything was left of them after the dust was gone.

John camped beneath his cart in another clearing, like the last in all respects except abandoned. It had been yanked out of the forest in exactly the same way as everything else: chop enough trees to get the hoist in, probe the ground, and sink the shaft. Stumps abounded. The good brown earth churned into striations of mud in red and black. Half-felled trees hung over half-planed logs. A creek flowed through and it ran with a black particulate sparkle and frothed a piss yellow. But John slept fine.

In the morning he dipped and climbed through the small, denuded hills around the mines. He left the scattered woods not long after and looked out over the flat, charred tobacco fields, then toward the white mansion where the man lived who had stuck Spanish Jim with that fancy knife. John did not know where to find the gray-eyed girl, but he thought someone living on that much of the earth was liable to know what was happening on smaller, nearby portions of it.

Rawls was out mending fences when he saw the boy on the mule cart in the distance approach the long drive between the cedars that led to Beauvais. He made his way toward the entrance, where another man was at the same job, arriving just after the boy on the cart.

"What say?" Rawls said by way of greeting.

The man rested an adze at his right shoulder, and with his left hand he held his hat and rubbed his forearm across his forehead as though the gesture might assist him in understanding the boy's nonsensical talk. "I don't know what he means, Rawls. He's talking something about he got a girl dog for a girl from around these parts and he wants to bring it to her. But I don't see no dog and he's pointing at that blanket wrapped up like a birthday present. I tried to tell him Mr. Levallois don't take to having no riffraff about."

The boy got down from his seat and began unwrapping the blanket. Rawls and the man looked at each other, neither having any idea what the boy was up to. A paw slipped out from the blanket's folds, speckled brown and white. "Aw hell, Rawls," the man hollered. "He's trying to tote a dead dog up to Miss Emily!"

John had by then unfolded the blanket as carefully as he could. The dog lay out on the blood-soaked blanket with her eyes looking emptily toward Richmond.

The man backed away until he tripped over the small collection of undressed cedar posts he had been working. He looked at Rawls and said, "No sir, no sir. I ain't messing with this damn business no more." Then he turned and jogged off up toward the other end of the fence that needed mending.

Shit, thought Rawls. This boy's got some fixation liable to get me in a hell of a mess. "All right now, feller," he said. "I'm gonna tell you, and I want you to listen real good now, nobody wants to look at something in a state like this."

But there was something in the boy's demeanor that he found pitiable. It was as if, despite whatever violent end had befallen this dog, with its mangled body slumping over the blanket like a house whose rotten beams had given up on standing, he was performing an act profound in both its sadness and its necessity, at least in the boy's own eyes. As Rawls tried to figure out how to get rid of him, something about the boy began to feel familiar, perhaps the dog, too, which he likely would have recognized more quickly if not for its disfigurement. Dumber than a box of hammers, this one, Rawls thought. And then he recalled having seen that face before, looking like it was permanently on the precipice of discovering that the true nature of the world was one of sadness and isolation, even when surrounded by those we love. The dull, glazed-over eyes, the mouth open and askew. The boy's breath continuing to pass over his tongue with a shallow regularity. The grass Rawls had hidden in at the ferry landing so long before. The firelight reflecting in the rippling James. Nurse gone out over the ice. Him desperate to find her but finding only further desperation. "I know you, boy?" asked Rawls.

"Might do," John answered. "Sometimes folks say they

know me, but I ain't strong on telling one black feller from another."

"You were down at the ferry landing with that old Melungeon when he got killed?"

"He was gonna teach me how to work the bateau," said John flatly.

"I understand most folks took him for a decent feller," Rawls said.

John's mouth remained open. He blinked a few times in quick succession as if waking up, his face otherwise expressionless. Rawls saw the blood caked like rust on the back of his shirt when the boy shifted in the seat.

"That blood on you from that dog there?" Rawls asked.

"No. I was down south of here, going about my picking. Feller I come across gets riled up and put the knife on me. Shot the dog." John turned away from Rawls, gathered the hair at the back of his neck, and showed him the wound the boy had given him.

"Damn, you wrapped that dog up like a present but didn't think to put nothing on that cut?"

"Well, some folks says..."

"Hush, let me see it now." Rawls gently traced his fingers over the ugly injury. What had likely been a wound as straight as a surveyor's mark was becoming ragged. It was hard to tell exactly what needed tending to with all the dirt. Rawls thought the boy hadn't washed in months, maybe longer, and he smelled like it. He took a rag out of his pocket and wiped the dirt off the back of John's neck as best he could without aggravating the wound. Here the blood congealed and brought the opposing bits of skin together, there pus pushed the wound apart. "You know you leave a cut like this it's liable to put you in the ground?"

"Ain't never been sliced up before."

"I'm gonna get you looked over so as you don't drop dead a week from now and come back to haunt my conscience," Rawls said. "And then we're going to bury that dog."

Men like Colonel Tom Fitzgerald rarely came to that part of Virginia before the war, but just as Rawls and John Talbot set their last shovelfuls of dirt over the bird dog Emily Reid had affectionately named Champion in her peaceful girl-hood, the young staff officer from Fall River, Massachusetts, ducked through the opening of his tent and looked out over the scattered fields and stands of pines beyond the church-yard where he'd slept. A runner interrupted his morning coffee with a message from his higher-ups requesting that he head to Washington immediately.

Ten years before or ten years after this peculiar time in history, it might have seemed odd to even the most casual observer that a man as young as Colonel Thomas Jefferson Fitzgerald had been assigned the governance of an area as large as the county. The best estimate, according to survey-ors, was that he, at barely twenty-two years old, was now for all intents and purposes the single sovereign of 423 square miles of rebellious territory between the James River to the north and the Appomattox River to the south. But such are the peculiarities of history that it did not seem particularly strange to anyone at all that day in late April of 1865 when he arrived by train in the ruins of Richmond, walked from the station into the street to a waiting horse, and began the ride a few hours farther south to the abandoned courthouse that would serve as the seat of his new administration. It did not seem strange to those who saw such a young man riding over the road toward the courthouse, because we measure strangeness not against what used to be or what will happen further out in time but rather against what we are accustomed to. And the residents of the county had known for many years now that if a man was needed for this role or that role, it should be no surprise that he might be very young or very old or very short or very tall. We draw water from whatever well we have, perhaps someone would have said, however small, for our needs can still be met by diminished things, even if that need is order. And anyway, whatever surprise the residents of that afflicted land had left would for a long time be quietly reserved for the fact that anyone still lived at all.

If any man was suited to this position in the Bureau of Refugees, Freedmen and Abandoned Lands, it was Colonel Fitzgerald, his superiors had said, for he had always exhibited a most scrupulous and just nature in all things, and wouldn't it be a harmonious conclusion for him to end the war very near to where he had begun it, those four long years before? On the train south, as the pinewoods outside his window broke from time to time on open field, a ruined farm, and then a bridge pulled down and now nearly built again, he thought about the way that everything that governed him had been reduced to scaffolding. Rules and what would be permitted he could comprehend, so he had stopped investing in the heavy load of right and wrong. Good and bad alike, he had lain down. He could even remember when.

Like many of his fellow officers, his commission had been given to him by chance, or in Tom Fitzgerald's eyes, it was given as the by-product of a system operating beyond its capacity. They had marched for weeks throughout the South, destroying anything that could be considered a means by which the rebels could survive. He himself had shot and butchered a dozen hogs, set the lit torch to tobacco fields and houses large and small, hung both Confederates and deserting Federals from the highest branch of the nearest tree until all the land was wasted, root to tip. Along the way many of his companions died, of wounds or sickness or one rising out of the other, and they were often left to expire among the little nubs of the fields they marched through, too sick themselves to remember anything like dignity in death.

But then they'd arrived at what seemed to be an untouched parcel, a house still stood with grace atop the hill, a line of linens blowing in the breeze like a hundred flags of truce. And the men who remained were set upon this house like an antiseptic. The officer in charge stood with his arms crossed, a mild perturbation on his face as the screams reached out to them from the house. The horses loosed and shot for sport. A teenage girl was stripped to her underthings and chased into a barn where she held off her attackers with a pitchfork while she could. And Tom, trying to find an argument that he could make about the rights and wrongs of war that would survive the derision of a half-a-hundred men maddened by so many years of having all their insight and introspection proved useless and therefore stripped away, settled on this: he said, "This is not permitted, sir."

And the officer merely laughed and said, "Go on, Fitzgerald, you go get some, too."

Tom, considering for a moment the nuances of the laws of war, finally said, "All right, then," and put his hand on the officer's hip, and pulled the man's pistol out, and shot him in the forehead with it. He had to shoot two other men who were determined to have their way with the girl. When everything had settled down, he said to the men now circling around him like a congregation, "There's what we can do and what we can't." And he nodded to a dozen more who still held torches on the porch. "We have our orders. Burn it. Burn it all," he said.

When they left the farm it was indistinguishable from every other they had seen and all that they would come to see, for they were an equalizing force in the world, and the figures in the half-remaining light that they had left behind were dumb with what will sometimes pass for justice on this earth, and poor now, and resigned to suffer like everyone else. And Tom was calm and light and felt he understood his role with a new clarity, and it was exact and pure and without mercy.

Such were the mysteries contained invisibly within the figure of the man atop the horse, dark haired and plainly dressed, his uniforms stored in the closet of a boarding-house up north as he made his way down the dusty turnpike to his unseen lodgings in the county courthouse. And he thought, as he pushed the horse beyond a few buildings gathered at a crossroad, that everyone he passed was more or less like him in every way but those that would be visible, and how easy it would be to let those things dictate the way they should be governed. But no, he had had experience, and so had they, and they were just like he was, after all, were they not, but with other rules and customs that they lived by. Who was he to say what should be done with them, or that he would not himself be a different man if he'd been given different rules? By this time he had gotten off his horse and spun the reins around a post planted in the ground before the courthouse. It was in a sad state of repair. But he reminded himself that he was not here to punish anyone. Perhaps some of them deserved punishment, certainly some did, for if the rules provided for that eventuality one could assume it was because someone would deserve it. But it was not his place to punish them. He was but a vehicle through which new rules would be established and enforced, a preacher of simplicity and clarity, an evangelist for perfect and unchanging order.

He stepped onto the porch of the modest courthouse. A few simple posts held up the cedar roof. Next door a squat jail protruded from the grass like an accident in granite. His office was simply appointed in a way that he had no fundamental desire to make significant alterations to; a chair and a wooden desk appeared as if made for outsize children, a portrait of Jefferson Davis hung above a rather overly ornamental mantel. Next to a window, another painting, of William Byrd II, hung askew, though it was hard to see clearly in the glare of western light flooding the window the afternoon of his arrival. He was alone. Staff and other functionaries would follow. Teachers were to be hired from among the local population when possible. Disputes of all kinds would be brought before him to be adjudicated. He was the law. And though he had the same doubts all men have about their own abilities, and was perhaps more honest about them than most, he considered this an improvement over what had qualified as the law before: its absence. The portrait of Davis he took down from the mantel and turned against the wall so that he would not have to look at him. The one of Byrd seemed less immediately offensive, and so he left it to look out in bemusement over his attempts to return this county to the nation.

His first visitor arrived that afternoon. Sheriff Pete Rivers entered his office without announcement, casually dragging an armchair until it was positioned before the desk opposite where Tom sat. Tom looked up curiously from his reading, an assessment of the county's particulars drawn up for him by a clerk at the War Department. The man across from him appeared wholly unremarkable. A bit fat. Probably twenty years older than himself. His greasy hair gray at the temples under the hat he noticeably neglected to remove upon entering the building. By the time the man rested the entirety of his weight into the upholstered chair and put his feet up on the corner of the desk, Tom's pistol was cocked and pointing at him from where it sat like a paperweight on the neatly organized stack of documents that had, mere moments before, occupied the full weight of the young colonel's attention.

"Shit!" the man shouted, jumping up from his seat. "You gonna shoot me down before you know who I am?"

"I very well may," said Tom.

"I'm the goddamn sheriff of this place!"

"What place would that be?"

"Wha–what?" Rivers stammered. "I'm the duly appointed law of Chesterfield County."

"Your authority has been revoked."

"Hell it has. I have jurisdiction over matters both, over matters..." It was nearly May, and not yet warm, but the exertion of jumping out of his chair compounded with his efforts to recall the exact formulation of his responsibilities had caused him to sweat profusely. "Over matters both civil and criminal."

"Had."

"What?"

"Had, I said. Past tense."

"Now, sir. Lookit. I'd bet I was the first man round these parts to take Lincoln's amnesty oath."

"I'll bet you were, too." He looked to Tom like a man with flexible convictions.

"And I ain't never took up arms against no Yankee like you in my life."

"I can tell. And I think we can both agree it would have ended poorly for you if you had, evidenced by my pistol ready on this desk and yours sitting in that holster. Just so we're both absolutely clear, my name is Colonel Thomas Fitzgerald. Lee has surrendered. You are not now the duly appointed law of anything. You are a man living in occupied territory, and if you enter my office armed again, I will kill you."

"Some bedside manner you have," Sheriff Rivers said, sinking into the chair.

"I'm not here to heal you," Tom answered. "Get to your business."

"I'm just carrying a message."

Tom extended his left hand with the palm up out over the desk.

Rivers saw that there was a slight tremor in both the hand and the young officer's left eye. The right hand, however, lay relaxed on the table, comfortably within the orbit of the pistol's wooden grip. He handed over the letter Levallois had given to him to deliver.

"Thank you," Tom said, returning the pistol to his holster and using a delicate silver letter opener to attend to the letter.

Rivers waited for the man to say something else, but he did not, so he turned to leave, pausing at the doorway to say, "I don't want you to take this the wrong way, Mr. Fitzgerald, but you'd do well to remember something."

Tom lifted his eyes slightly above the top of the paper from which he had been reading, annoyed by the disregard with which this Rivers fellow treated his time. "And what might that be?" he asked.

"Somewhere on this earth," the former sheriff said, "I'm sure there are people who love you. But they ain't here."

The following day Fitzgerald saddled his horse and left the courthouse in the care of a trusted sergeant. The directions to Beauvais were straightforward enough. Prior to his arrival, he'd made notations on his maps of the locations of the homes of prominent Confederates and important men who would soon fall under his purview, and when the locals saw him seemingly staring blankly out from beneath his broad cavalryman's hat, none of them could see the purpose in his gaze, that he was amending his understanding of the land and refining the plan with which he intended to rejoin it to the nation.

He was aware, of course, that he remained at least in theoretical danger. When told that his superiors in Washington suggested he ride out to make his assessments under arms, perhaps with ten or twenty good men, he said he would take it under advisement. Tom did not think there were ten or twenty good men left in the world, and that limiting the pool of candidates to those serving in the army would reduce his chances of finding even one to almost nil. And anyway, he thought, he'd faced rebs who were actually suited to killing and was still standing. So with a soldier's practical fatalism he decided to conserve his bureaucratic resources for other matters.

As he rode it occurred to him he had not seen a wild

thing run or fly since arriving in Virginia. In his boyhood he would watch the smoke-gray breakers surrender to the wind and die along the stony shores of Narragansett Bay. Once, on a bright warm July day, he'd spent hours watching a humpback breach and dance its way out toward the Atlantic. He stayed sprawled along a shoreline rock until the great beast was far too distant to observe, and stayed longer until night fell. When, finally, everything around him was cool and quiet and blue-black except the stars, he began to weep. He was inconsolable even as winter arrived, though he was not sure why. Sometimes he'd ponder the giant icicles that hung precipitously from the eaves of the textile mills crowding the banks of the Quequechan River, vaguely hopeful that one or more would fall on him. It seems that the creatures of this earth only withdraw from exceptional acts of violence: that of a land surrendered wholly to industry, or war on a scale that is its equal. They are, for the most part, indifferent to its more private and quotidian manifestations that occur everywhere on earth: a nighttime whipping in a lamplit barn, a hand snuffing out a desperate cry behind a bedroom's locked door. So it must be said that his ride to Beauvais astounded him, filled as it was with the nuthatches' song, a doe bleating in distress as a group of whitetails sprang erect and dashed into the trees, the cares of every living thing contentedly reserved for the unique harm that each was wedded to from birth. Something revived in him that had been diminished for a long time. When his regiment first headed south what seemed like a million years before, he'd brought along a journal to record something of the natural world in its blank pages. But nothing was ever recorded, his pen captured no exotic animals, and he had not bothered to describe or sketch the flora that turned late April in the South into a riot of light and color. He came out of the war feeling as though he'd emerged from a dream he could hardly remember. And the book remained marked only by its emptiness.

And so much still seemed unrecoverable to him. His parents were dead, though he did not know it. They had been buried, over the course of the more than three years he'd been gone, between and among the graves of Portuguese immigrants who'd died of influenza, hunger, homesickness, or some other fatal condition common to those far from home. Now their matching stones, alike in all but name and dates of birth and death, broke up the regularity of the graveyard's register: Silva, Almeida, Fernandes, Fitzgerald, Antunes, Reis, Marques. If he'd ever made it back, the colonel might have said that Fall River would never be the same. But he did not make it back; only a few of his letters did. And even these sat undelivered on the desk of the aging postman, who woke from his afternoon nap and opened them, perhaps reading them quietly before the light of his kitchen stove, *From your beloved son, somewhere in Georgia or Tennessee,* followed by a description of the letter writer's dreams, *Mother, all night long I dream of running but being too slow,* or the next from outside Petersburg, *Mother, all night long I dream of being caught, of throwing punches with no force,* or from North Carolina, *Mother, in my dreams it is always dark and my teeth fall out.* When the postman read the first of these he began to feel a deep but unspecific sorrow that only increased throughout the afternoon, something to do with, as he would say to his wife that evening, the fact that thoughts like these must ever get recorded at all.

TEN

GEORGE POINTED OUT the way to Lottie the best he could. The car complained about the bumps and ruts in the road the whole drive east toward Lumberton. He had only flashes of the old life he'd left behind to draw on. But there was such familiarity, too. The smell of a place never changes, he thought, and somewhere deep in his being he felt the dark waters return to him, and the moss hung like garlands from the cypress trees as if to welcome him. They drove along old washboard roads he thought he recognized. He whistled. High summer light still fell between the leaves. "We're out back of behind now, girl," he said. His wheezing had gotten worse during the storm that passed over as they left the theater.

"You okay, Mr. Seldom?" Lottie asked.

"It's just the weather."

They took wrong turns, running into dead ends that dissolved into the fringes of the swamps, and while they searched, the sun set over the black river through the trees. Hours later, the moon hung full and bright in the cloudless night. "It's got to be nearby," George said. They sat for a while on the side of another back road with the car idling, and when they drove on, he asked her to turn the car down an overgrown path. The wheels followed along imperfectly in grooves as deep as wagon ruts. They reached the trail's end, and before them in the car's high beams stood a cabin in the depths of disrepair. Lottie threw the shifter up into PARK on the steering column. George opened the passenger door and she came around to help him out of the car.

"Is this it, Mr. Seldom?" she asked.

He stared at the place and nodded.

More than seventy-five years had passed since he'd seen it. The years had made their mark on the place. A home requires living in to deserve the name. It is as if shouts and reconciliations provide a barrier against both time and weather. For a floor to truly be kept clean, the stomping of a child's bare feet must dirty it first. A porch roof caves in more quickly when there is no one to sit beneath it waiting for a loved one to return. And this cabin had missed all of those happenings for many years.

The door was buried under the remains of the porch. They walked around it, looking for a place to enter, but could not find one. The walls tilted precariously. The roof had several holes in it. George saw buckets full of moonlight pour through them when he cupped his hands around his eyes and peered into one of the last windows to have glass within its frame.

George walked back to the front of the cabin, wheezed

again, and sat heavily on a tree stump in the cleared dooryard.

Lottie went to him and put her hand on his shoulder. The old man began to cry. All his anger and disappointments seemed as though they meant to shoot out of his body, from every pore and every angle. The old man shook desperately. In that moment George thought his whole life had been a failed effort to guard against the grief that came for him now. Something summoned him. Lottie knelt on the ground next to him and wrapped her small arms around his waist. She did not talk. George felt her arms around his waist and it was hard for him to tell if she was pulling him toward or away from whatever it was that called to him.

All the rooms in the crumbling building of his memory began to reconstruct themselves. He heard his own voice, higher pitched and unweathered by time, echoing through the tumbledown house. In his mind it was still the nineteenth century, and in that century he wept and raged on his bed. The woman tried to console him but could not.

"Who is my father?" he asked her.

"I don't know," the old woman said.

"My mother?"

"It's hard to say, though I know that she could read and write. She was probably very beautiful, as you sometimes have a look about you that I am sure belonged to her face first." She was on her knees behind him, rubbing the back of the boy who had been left to her an innocent, and who now felt an intense, pitiless confusion, surely a close relative of experience and grief. "George," she said, "someone loved you very much. Just as I do. Enough that they cared for you more than themselves."

"How do I know he was not a bad man?"

"I can't promise you either way. But what I know is that it's common for a good man to be fatherless. There are times when a young man chases something in his father, and the chasing turns him bad. They aim themselves at the world like a rifle. But you won't have to chase that thing. You have been loved so well, and by so many, even if it is beyond your recollection."

It was true, both that he was loved and that he would not have a single thing to chase. He left the house and never returned. And he never again saw the woman who raised him. As he walked away from her that day, leaving behind the moss in the cypress trees and the black water of the Lumber River, he had no place at which to aim himself. So instead he searched, not knowing that what it was he hoped to find had been there always, at times still tasting the river's bitter tannins in his mouth.

He came back to Lottie. He gently pulled her hands from around his waist and stood her up. "I'll be all right now, I think. Woman who lived in this house loved me better than anyone I ever knew, but it was too late to tell her that I knew it by the time I knew it for sure." He did not know why, but he thought the girl might have answers to his questions. "Is that a terrible thing?" he asked the girl.

"I don't think it is," she said. "I think maybe sometimes a thing is so true its being said don't make a difference at all." Lottie did not know what made a person good, or if she was such a person herself, but it seemed to her that if this man was not, then we ought not use the word anymore. She recalled her mother scolding her earlier for insisting on involving herself in the man's life. And now she stood before him, a little afraid of what was happening, but the fact that George did not seem scared gave her some comfort. The old man remained on the stump. She was not sure if he had heard anything she'd said. She desperately hoped he had heard her, and though she felt with an unusual certainty that her mother and grandmother would be disappointed if he hadn't, she did not say those things again. His head leaned down. He began to breathe heavily, but with diminishing returns. Each time he exhaled, he breathed out more than he had taken in. Or so it seemed to Lottie. She did not know how long she stood there. She felt hypnotized, but then awoke.

As he left, George's grief for himself was replaced by a grieving for the world. He felt as though he knew all the names that had come before him and all that would follow. He put the names on his breath and with each exhalation he said them in a language beyond speech. Lottie folded her hands into the shape of a cup and she put the cup under his mouth. He exhaled once more, and filled the cup. Lottie let the silence surround her. George said all the names and then was gone.

ELEVEN

ANYONE NEAR THE boundaries of Beauvais Plantation, as April turned to May in 1865, would have seen the passing into history of ten thousand things. Things with names that had been carried all throughout the indifferent progress of time. But winter had returned to the county like a guest who had forgotten her coat, and a cold rain fell, and a gray mist pressed up against the trees aligned in windbreaks along the road. And the road, too, lay obscured in mist and rain, so even those who traveled on it might have missed the reliability of its direction, as if all sense of time and place had been obscured by some premonition of smoke that slinked over the grounds. They might miss each thing as it transformed into ash and disappeared, miss the way that names were left behind without anything to carry them, or a reason to be carried.

The weather had turned quickly, and Colonel Tom Fitzgerald seemed to bring it with him to Beauvais when he pulled his horse's reins and turned down between the rows of cedars toward the house. Nurse was under a stable eave to stay dry. She beat the little ones' dirty nappies on a washboard and watched him come. "You see that man riding this way, Rawls?" she said.

Rawls was under the eave, too, and he had been happily watching young George toddle about despite the weather. The Levallois twins lay napping in a wicker bassinet that Rawls and John Talbot had built for them the previous week, and Rawls reached over to set the bassinet rocking, always thinking that the girls must be sickly, their skin such a fragile-looking color, not even a color, really, with eyes so big and blue that he was afraid they might go blind at any moment and Nurse would be saddled with the blame. "I do," he said.

The man approached and then stopped his horse. Rain fell down the brim of his hat in curtains that obscured his face. Rawls saw the butt end of a big pistol hanging out of a leather holster. The holster seemed well worn and so did the saddle and the tie-down martingale, too, and Rawls had the impression that the man would also appear thoroughly broken in if he could only see his face well enough to say for sure. Rawls stilled the gently rocking bassinet with his hand. Nurse set the washing down. The man spoke softly, and in the racket of gray weather he was hard to hear, so Rawls stepped to the edge of the eave of the stable roof where the rain fell in a great sheet between them. He made sure to place himself between the children and the rider.

"This is Beauvais," the man said.

It did not seem to Rawls that the man was asking, but by

the way he lingered on the horse in the rain, Rawls decided he was waiting on an answer. "It is."

"Tell me. What's he like, this Levallois?"

"I don't know that I can tell you more than anyone else could," Rawls said, suspicious of the man's intentions but certain that Virginia was not yet a place where he, freeman or slave, could keep his opinions to himself when asked about them.

"Nevertheless. You are the one I asked."

"He's the boss around these parts."

"Of this place, you mean?"

"Sure, this place. But he's got interests all over."

"All over the county?" the colonel asked.

"Yes, sir. Most of the fields. Big stake in the mines. The niggers in the fields. The niggers in the mines. White folks in both. The store. The station. Railroad what going in a little south of here."

"Is he a reasonable man?" asked the colonel.

"I don't claim to know the workings of his mind," said Rawls.

The colonel dismounted and tied the reins to a post holding up the eave under which Nurse and Rawls and the three young children were staying dry. He introduced himself to both of them. Nurse rose and curtseyed and he shook Rawls's hand and did not acknowledge the young ones. He told them he was with the U.S. government, and that things were going to change down south.

"From what to what?" Rawls asked. He was not often in the position of asking white men questions, and so he made room for the man to come under the eave to get out of the weather, but the man did not.

"We're going to be one country again," he answered Rawls.

"That's a nice thing to hear, but I don't think most fellers will notice."

"Yes. I suspect there might be difficulties," he said. "A lot of rebels came out of Chesterfield. But where a man comes from never meant much to me. I killed graybacks by the cartload no matter where they were from, as I was told to do. And now I am told to make sure things go as cordially as possible." Tom could not always recognize how worn and tattered his sense of decorum had become. He had not meant to offend the woman, and said so, and Nurse and Rawls looked at each other as though they might laugh, but they did not.

"We are grateful for you," she said. She meant her words of gratitude toward the man standing in the rain, but she also meant that very often the world is cruel, as he must know, and decorating the world does not disguise its cruelty; it simply digs its foundations deeper. She had once told Rawls of the night at Chimborazo when she dreamed of the endless line of lanterns headed out toward Oakwood Cemetery, how she had dug the graves herself. And Nurse did not think that she had dreamed of this man, standing right in front of her. Yet here he was anyway, telling her without adornment that what she'd only dreamed of, he had lived.

Tom felt a great shame come over him when he described the change in his instructions. He thought evil men ought to be killed. The deaths of evil men were worthy of celebration. And weren't these rebels evil? He had seen the cheeks of their little children flushed pink with rage, the prettily made-up faces of their staid wives turned joyful with bloodlust. And there was precedent, too, for hadn't God marked Cain? And who had fired the first shot, breaking an injunction carved in stone on his holy mountain? Now they called for reconciliation. Cain would neither wander nor be marked but would sit right down again at the table and ask you to pass the jam. Sometimes Tom allowed himself to think it wasn't right. But it was dangerous for him to think this way, as his grip on himself was only strong when it reached out for order, an order that had more in common with a river carving a path through a valley or high mountains turned forever into dust. An inevitable order, rather than one invented by old, fat cowards who put the world together like a puzzle in their wood-paneled rooms in Washington. He had not heard Nurse speak. He turned away from them, toward the colonnaded porch, and left wordlessly.

Levallois watched from the window of the library. He's come as called, he thought. He considered it a victory, as he often mistook inevitabilities for evidence that the world still bent to his will. When the colonel entered, Levallois sized him up. A young man, he thought, and inexperienced. Probably harmless, but worth keeping an eye on nonetheless. He stood to greet his guest. "I'm so glad you've arrived safely. It must be quite perilous down here for a man like you," he said. Levallois could be a charming man when he wanted to, but the colonel was not charmed. Two men have rarely been so distant in their assessments of each other.

"I'm fine. Your man out there says you have a lot of sway in this county."

"Does he now?"

"You are paying wages, I expect."

"I have always valued good work. You can ask anyone."

"I will," the colonel said. "Do you know the duties I have been assigned to perform?" he asked.

Levallois poured out two snifters of brandy, set them on a side table below the Mercator map, and asked the officer to sit. "I'm afraid you'll have to be a little more specific. Please. Have a drink."

"I don't want anything," said Tom.

"Everybody wants something," said Levallois, smiling. "It's customary."

"You misunderstand me. I'm not here to abide by your rules. I am here to ensure that you will abide by the law."

Levallois poured both brandies into one glass and drank it down in a big swallow. "Ah," he said, still emboldened by his initial misapprehension of the man.

And it must be said that Tom suffered a misapprehension of his own regarding Levallois. He looked at the man holding his glass at the rim with the tips of his fingers. He thought that he had seen his type before. It was true. He had seen dozens of them, indolent and puritanical and greedy even for another man's free clean air to breathe. They were all the same. They dreamed their farms were kingdoms. As if a thousand acres of soybean, tobacco, or cotton, the dirt of which had never touched their hands, could make a man a king. The savages out west had more. Land so vast a man could not tame it in ten lifetimes. The Chinamen had more in their canopied jungles, and birds and beasts resident therein resisting all description. Yet these men always thought that they could dig their furrows into clay and resist a sovereignty so insistent upon itself that it made their protestations all the more ridiculous. He had been that insistence. And it always ended the same way. He would come into their stately mansions and they would talk, not of their families or of safety, but of abstractions. They would spit at his feet and say their honor was inviolable. They would swear no oath; they would make no acts of contrition. Sometimes Tom found it necessary to correct their misconceptions about what they would or would not do, and he would beat them with his fists until it was hard for him to tell if he was wet with their blood or his own sweat. He would take them outside to where the slaves were gathered, it almost always happened the same way, and he would say to the assembled crowds that they had been free people since the first day of 1863, and if this man had been a master since, then his crime called out for remedy. Silence followed, but once encouraged they would shout, "He whipped us against that cart," or "He shot Ed Jackson and let him rot nearby where the horses drink." Some variation on these themes. Tom would split the differences between them. In Georgia he dragged a master from his bed and hung him from a barn's crossbeam, his wife and little children begging for God's mercy. In Tennessee he shot one dead on his porch so the now-free people could see that what they had paid for in blood many times over would be repaid in kind. He would burn the big white houses down before he left, and a song always followed him.

But he was wrong about Levallois. He was of that type, but there is such variation within every category that they lose their utility much more quickly than most people imagine. "I took the oath already," Levallois said. "I'm not a planter anymore. I'm a businessman." With that, his crimes had been erased even if his sins had not. Now what he owned was not restricted to the boundaries of Beauvais. What he owned crossed those boundaries as if they were not there, and his property was no longer tied to any particular piece of ground but resided in a hundred different ledgers in a hundred different offices in a hundred different buildings in a hundred different cities, north and south. And so his pardon lived in all those places, too. "We're one country again," he said. "Won't you have a drink," he asked again. "After all, we only want what's fair."

Tom caught a glimpse of a boy outside the house carrying a rake. For a moment, he had mistaken the rake for a rifle and he followed the boy with his eyes, uncharacteristically turning his back to the seated man as the boy walked out of view. "I don't think you want what's fair," the colonel said. "To be fair I'd have to leave your world a ruin. Justice will have to do instead."

"Equality under the law," said Levallois. "That's all anybody down here wants. And peace. We get the papers, too. We've heard how vengeful the Grand Army has become.

Fair treatment. Nothing more." He could see he'd made the colonel uncomfortable. And while Levallois frequently depended on the advantages a man could find in the discomfort of others, he also knew how delicate a thing like discomfort could be.

Tom could feel himself trembling with temptation. It was as if Mr. Levallois was courting him, seducing him to act as he would have when the war was still on. His mind called to him through his rising anger, resisting the takeover of instinct and urge that he knew would soon be almost irresistible. But the voice in his mind called louder, and in an instant the colonel recognized he had allowed himself to be caught back-footed. He turned around quickly and saw that Levallois had stood and moved a step toward him, his hand moving in an erratic orbit around the knife sheathed on his belt. Tom lowered his open palm toward the back strap of his New Army Colt in a deliberate and precise trajectory.

"An unequivocal man, I see," said Levallois, raising his hands as if to indicate he was being misunderstood.

"Life's less complicated that way."

Levallois moved the marble table from between the two chairs and sat back down. He put his feet up on the chair opposite him and folded his hands over his belly. "What's this talk of ruin? It has no place in the modern world. What do you think we'll do if you leave us with nothing? All men have needs."

"You can have your memories."

"That might be worse for you than you think. But still you

believe you can come down here and rub our noses in shit like misbehaving puppies? It won't work."

"That doesn't mean you don't deserve it."

"You're right. It doesn't mean that. But it still won't work. Colonel, I was born in Virginia. I'll die in Virginia. I don't concern myself with right and wrong as they exist somewhere out in the ether, or in goddamn New England or wherever you come from. I'll do what's right for me and mine, right here, where I live. And so will everyone else, you included, where they live. Nothing changes but the names we give to things. You want to have a debate about justice? You're a young man yet, Colonel. Open your eyes. Tell me what it looks like. Come back in five years, in ten, in a hundred, and tell me what you've accomplished. In the meantime, I will take what I need."

"You will take what you want."

"You act like there's a man anywhere on earth who can tell the difference."

Emily had seen him coming, too. She was in her bedroom, where she passed most of her time now. She was not imprisoned. She was forgotten, but the results were more or less the same. Levallois had lost interest in her quite quickly after the wedding, his attentions almost exclusively reserved for the new railway line and the station being built atop her family's former land. And though she began to despise him almost as quickly as he seemed to forget her, his indifference inflamed her contempt more intensely each passing day. It transformed, until it and her disgust for her father's weakness and abandonment of her became concentrated into one idea: that the men of Beauvais Plantation were the sole impediment to the life of freedom and isolation she had come to long for. On a few occasions since the birth of her children, she had been forced to perform her wifely duties, though by then she could recognize herself as a substitute for her husband's true desires and muddle through disinterestedly. But his failures quickly turned to blame and accusation, and though she refused to accept the burden of this blame, this resistance had required a hardening of her heart to such an extent that Emily sometimes found herself surprised to feel it beating still. Even her daughters, helpless and innocent though they were, carried in their eyes the reflection of their father, and sometimes Emily withdrew from them because she could not bear how unpredictable her hatred of them was, these little blue-eyed dolls whom she imagined hissing at her when she turned her back.

Nurse had seen Emily earlier in the day, pacing the garden, stopping suddenly to place a pale hand over her chest. Her mistress then drew a quick and silent shock of air into her lungs. They caught each other's eyes, and Emily's mouth was formed into a delicate circle, as if made from glass. Nurse felt her face mirror her mistress's, in shock and fear and wonderment, for until that moment she was sure she had known the whole range of terrible emotion. But this was new, and when Nurse grabbed her skirts and turned to leave the garden in a rush, the image of her mistress's pale eyes stayed with her, ringed with tears quivering like mercury. Nurse was terrified that whatever caused those tears was not merely a sadness she had known herself, but instead the symptom of some unnamed illness that anyone near Emily might catch were they to get too close.

For Emily, life had become the walking of a post. At night she shuffled through the darkened hallways, as ghostly as a living girl could be, and Nurse soon enough discovered how frightful it can be to wake someone who does not know they are asleep. During the day, for an hour or two, she'd pace the boxwood garden while Nurse kept the children nearby in the yard, until her days turned into a performance. The motions of motherhood. Retiring to her room. A visit to her father for lunch in the overseer's house, where she'd listen to some machination or theory about how he would set the world right.

Bob had, with few exceptions, become a recluse, and Levallois tolerated his presence only out of a diminishing sense of obligation to his wife. But Bob had taken to the dullard Talbot. When Rawls first brought him up to the house to tend to his injury, he had raised the notion to Bob that the boy might be some kind of kin to Bob's deceased wife on account of their shared surname. And this idea, that John Talbot might be a connection to a part of his life he had left in the creek outside Mechanicsville, stuck in his mind the way a saw sticks in timber with a novice at the handle. He revised his past into a holy idyll. Made little plans and designs. And on those rare days when his daughter appeared, he would insist that the three of them take cold drinks on the stone porch of the house the world had conspired to exile him to, where the land rose up a little higher than the rest, and from which place he had watched the fires of Richmond paint a black streak across the northern sky only weeks before. Bob's pain was still fresh. The wounds, while healed, were not yet a year old. And his discovery of his clever dispossession by Levallois was only a few months in the past. As the weather warmed he filled the air with paranoiac talk. "Their day is coming, Emily," he would say, again and again. "Yes, Papa," she would say, dismissing him, as his bitter protestations had long since lost their bite. She did not think her father would know what to do with himself without his grievances. And she certainly didn't think he would ever try to have them redressed.

Cause and effect were too complex a set of principles for John. Levallois had been nervous to have him around at first when he saw Rawls tending to the boy's wound. Levallois was sure he saw a spark of recognition in the boy's eyes, but he did not see the change in demeanor he expected to accompany the spark. Once he caught the boy's gaze lingering on the antler handle of his knife. "You recall this knife, boy?" he asked cruelly. John replied that he did. When he offered no further comment, Levallois took the knife out and handed it to him, holding the blade in his palm and letting the carved end come to rest where John Talbot waited to grip it. He looked it over intently, but it did not occur to him to stick the blade right up under Levallois's ribs, over and over again until he was too tired to stand, and to continue until he had stabbed the man so many times he no longer screamed, until the man just sat there with his arms over his knees while the knife went in, grimacing occasionally and bleeding all over the brick floor, blowing out deep breaths as John Talbot punched the knife into his sides. He could have done it quite easily, as Levallois was not afraid of John, and it is easiest to kill a man who is not afraid of you because he'll let you do it. But this did not occur to him, even though he could recall with great detail how it had appeared when the man had done those very things to Spanish Jim, who had been born before the last century had come in, long before John's life had been reduced to a riddle he could find no satisfying answer to.

On some days after sitting with her father, Emily would allow John Talbot to accompany her as she walked the grounds of Beauvais. Being with him was very much like being alone, she thought. She felt unencumbered by obligation in his company. We are most real to ourselves, and surely this has been said before, so perhaps it is forgivable that Emily misunderstood his deficiencies as a kind of incompleteness. Someone else might have said it differently; that while Emily might know she was a child of God she did not yet know that she was not an only child.

Emily would lead John Talbot through the swinging garden gate and out through the broad green leaves and between the thousand knee-high hills of the tobacco fields. They went sometimes to sit beneath the old sycamore where the new railway line to Raleigh had a stop. Levallois Crossing, it was called, almost now a little town distinct from the rest of Chesterfield. And when Emily took John there, she did not see signs of progress in the steam plume of the engine as it roared and dove backward between the trees along the rails. She saw only that which should be hers, that which she refused to leave no matter how desperately she wanted to escape. Levallois had declared he would drag the whole of the county into the present day, and he had. Her father kept insisting he would make things right. But her father was a wrecked loon. Her mother lay buried in a grave they'd had to put a fence around so that business-men heading north and south would not piss on it before the conductor called for all aboard. She saw her husband's lawyers coming and going from the library at Beauvais. How they clutched signed papers to their chests and shuf-fled out with an urgency that seemed to her ridiculous, as if the ownership of a quarter point of interest could be the thing on which the world depended. And so in those early days after the war ended, Emily decided that the freedom she had secured for herself in the innermost workings of her mind and heart was not enough, and she would never know more than that unless she acted.

One day, when summer stirred the wet air like a broth, they passed through the woods and into the high wild meadows, John behind her as she darted and zagged through the chest-high grass. Emily was now intensely focused on their destination, and she did not see that underfoot were the husks of a billion wingless nymphs. John noticed, but said nothing, not thinking there was cause to comment on it, though he had never seen a sight like that before that he could recall. He accepted the world as it was quite easily, as his mind created no alternatives for either improvement or diminishment, and so he did not lose himself in frustrated ambitions or the confusions of category. When a man has a choice and yet abstains from the ruination of whatever little piece of the earth he can alter, he is called a good man. If it comes as naturally to him as breathing, we call him a simpleton. But such is life. John rubbed at the scar on the back of his neck. He watched Emily dart into a stand of cedars, and toward the road that led down to the river. When she was out of sight he was struck deaf by a high electric rattle and buzz, and blinded by a cloud of locusts rising from the meadow. It seemed to John that the earth had taken wing as if to flee from itself. He walked through the cloud, parting the swarming bugs with his outstretched hands. They covered him over completely, occupying every inch of the meadow and raising a terrific noise, but he was not afraid. It seemed to John like a kind of music. Their wings beat the air, beautifully. Emily was far away. He did not know how much time had passed. He thought that he would tell her about what he had seen, but by the time he found her sitting on the bank the locusts had lost their novelty, had become but another piece of the common world, and so he did not tell her, and she was not reminded of her terrible dreams.

She sat on a large rock out in the shallows. John settled onto the bank, hanging his legs over a knot of roots from which a spring flood had washed away the dirt. They had not talked at all. They rarely did. He had told her about the dog after he and Rawls had buried it, even though Rawls had asked him not to. It was hard for him to be dishonest. Rawls had tried to explain to him that sometimes the truth makes life harder for people, and that both the truth and lies come in different flavors. He said you can pardon yourself if you have to hold the truth back on occasion, and since it would be a hard day today, and a harder one tomorrow, why add to the difficulties of another if it could be prevented just by keeping one's mouth shut? John was sure Rawls was a good man, and he liked his company, and he liked to be asked by Rawls for his assistance on one project or another around Beauvais, but he also was confused by the world he described, and the careful steps one had to take to walk through it. John had no head for lies of any variety. And so he told Emily what had happened to the dog whose name he could not recall, the one that had kept him warm at night while he wandered Virginia, living off its scraps. And he now followed her the way he imagined the dog had, trying to take its place for Emily as if this might be a kind of atonement, always trying to be mindful that he must protect her from harm, like the harm the boy with the broken glasses had brought on him and the dog both.

Out on her gray perch she watched the slate-blue water course and roil over the midstream stones. Herons dove for shad and barked. She felt John near her on the bank, careless. She felt a great, untapped power circulating through her body, some force that had accrued with every lingering stare that her clouded eyes had caught and turned away throughout her life. And there was nothing more to do but harness it. She had been a dutiful wife. She had listened to her husband. He talked as though he were singularly endowed with the ability to see the true nature of the world. People can be relied upon so well to show you the right course if only you want to see it, he often said. Yes, she thought. That was true. She slipped off her clothes, taking her time with it, and slid into the water. John stared, just as she thought he would. His mouth was open. She asked if he would join her.

She steered him to a patch of moss on the riverbank after they swam and then climbed on top of him. Afterward they lay together in the grass. John did not talk. Months had passed since his return. She had guided him all the while. Correcting him whenever he said something that was not right, sometimes harshly, but always with a touch or gesture after to ease the sadness that her harshness brought him. He began to see the world the way she told him it ought to be seen, and John felt his life beginning to take a smooth, effortless course, until her ideas about the world replaced the few that had been his own.

Emily said she was sure that he was meant to find her again. How good it was to have turned the tragedy of their first meeting into the bond they now shared. "I'll rely on you now, John," she said. "Levallois is cruel and cold. Look how he treats my father, left in the overseer's house like it's a prison. Think of what he did to the ferryman."

"To Spanish Jim," said John. "He cut him up good. I used to look for him even though I remember letting him in the water. I put some right big rocks in his pockets first. The dog was there. But I'd look for him some. In pictures. When I'd find little tintypes and things I'd look to see if he were in the pictures."

"Such a terrible man. I can't bear to think of how it must torment you. To have to see him living so comfortably while you are left with only scraps and memories."

John did not know the meaning of torment, but he did not ask Emily, as he did not want her to part with him for not knowing the meanings of words as well as she did. He did not want her to part with him ever again. He wanted to swim with her and lie together in the grass forever. "I love you," he said.

She smiled and turned toward him and put her hand on his cheek. He shivered. Emily laughed. "That means someone has walked over the place your grave will be," she said.

"Should I say it again?" he asked.

"Oh, John," she said. "You must be careful with that word because it means so much." How easy it was to lead him where she wanted him to go, she thought. Emily wondered if all men were this way, or just boys like John, as eager and uncertain in this as he was in everything. She thought of Levallois's weight on her. She worked to hide her disgust. "Sometimes it's true when people say it and sometimes it's just a word."

John Talbot was confused. Why did she think he would say it if it were not true? "I don't know what else to call it," he said.

"Familiarity," she said.

"I ain't studied that word," said John.

She laughed again and John was sure that he did love her. She kissed him.

"It means that maybe you only think you love me and are really only used to me. I don't want to think that's what you mean."

"I guess that's partly what I mean, but the rest, too."

"I don't want it to be just a word when you say it to me, John."

"How do I make it so you know it's true?"

She rolled away from him and looked up to the crowns of the trees hanging over the river. Out of the corner of her eye she could see that he was racked with thought, desperate to please her but unsure how. She smiled to herself. She clasped his hand in both of hers. Light retreated from them as the sun fell westward. The sky as red now as a slaughter-house floor. "When love is a true thing, John, you do not need the word," she said. "You only need a demonstration."

TWELVE

BILLY RIVERS FOUND his wife in the tub on the second weekend of March 1985. On some evenings Lottie would take a bath after they ate their late dinner, then went to sit on their nylon chairs above the riprap where they'd watch the bay. If she had done a lot of work in her studio earlier in the day, she would often get quite dirty, and so Billy did not think much of the fact that she had been in the bathroom for nearly an hour. He did not worry until he heard the broadcast of the ball game end and another show begin. Lottie never had much use for television. She preferred music. And while there was always some old country song or another coming out of the garage while she was in there, Billy didn't think he'd ever heard the TV on in the house unless a Georgetown game was on. She had a little RCA portable she'd bought from Mr. Mathew's Electronorama out on 33 a few years back, with a black-and-white screen on one side and a radio on the other, and she'd tote it around to have the country station playing, but if there was a Georgetown game on you could bet she'd have the TV going. You'd hear the click of the knob and then a slow pulsing hum and then maybe a few straining bars of the fight song, all the voices singing "Lie down forever, lie down," to which Lottie would hum along.

Lottie would sit in the dark and watch the flicker of the Big East game of the week. She'd place the small RCA set on a shelf in her studio or out on the screened-in porch or rigged up with a hairbrush and a towel to support it on the bathroom sink. She appreciated the young men's perseverance in the face of the impossibility of perfection: the squeak of sneakers on a wood floor, a ball hanging in the air against its backspin, the rough jostling toward life under the net. She had never lived in a place that had a top-tier basketball team, of course, but almost by accident she had developed an abiding affection for Georgetown, which seemed near enough to Deltaville for her to claim. And she had come to love the way the young men in gray never stooped for consolation, and never bawled or yawped when the victories they expected came.

But on that night, after midnight had come and gone, Billy heard the theme song for *Falcon Crest* replace the sounds of the game after it ended and began to worry. He went to the door and knocked. She'd thrown a towel over the top of the door when she'd gone in, so the door was cracked open, and he heard the television going on the sink and nothing else. No splashing. No humming the way she sometimes would. "You all right in there, Lot?" he called from the other side of the door. He pushed it open when she didn't answer. The only source of light was the TV set.

Two aromatic candles she'd lit and set on the rim of the tub had burned down to almost nothing, the wax liquefied completely and then re-formed. The pale light from the TV fell smoothly over Lottie's naked body in the tub.

Billy knew she wasn't dead. He'd lived for fifteen years with ghosts. Death is a white pall. Color runs from the body quickly when death comes to it, and Lottie still had the dark flush of life on her skin. But he did not hear her breath. He pulled her out of the tub. Water splashed all over him and all over the floor. The candles fell to the floor and cracked a tile. The television was still on. Billy pulled her out of the bathroom and laid her on the floor. His mind spun automatically through a checklist: responsiveness, breathing, bleeding…He slapped her cheeks lightly and called her name. "Lottie, girl. C'mon, girl, wake up, baby." He slapped her cheeks harder. He leaned down and let his ear hover just above her mouth, listening for a whisper of breath, waiting to feel the air touch his skin. It took him less than a minute to get her wrapped in a blanket and into his truck. The motor fired right up. They kicked up so much dust on the gravel road that it obscured the moon.

She regained consciousness as they crossed the White Stone Bridge over the Rappahannock River. Billy had the hammer down, and she looked at the speedometer as it waved above one hundred. "It's all right, Billy. Ease it back some, hon," she said.

He looked over at her. His eyes were big as turning wheels behind his glasses and wet with tears. "We'll be at the hospital soon," he said.

"I know how well you look after little things like this. It's just a little thing."

He wondered how long she'd known. Some mornings he would get into the shower and see small spatters of blood around the drain. He thought it looked like rust at first. Hard water, maybe. He had not seen blood outside his dreams in a long time.

"A little thing?" he asked.

"It'll be okay, Billy."

"Will it?"

"Sure." A little quiet passed between them. "You're a good man, Billy," she said.

He did not tell her that he did not think it was true. It wasn't a lie. She had never lied to him, and never would. But he thought that she was wrong. They crossed over the water and onto land again. The bridge and its tangle of iron trusses were far behind them in the dark. Billy beat his hand on the steering wheel and cursed the heavens.

Billy left her bedside only once before she was officially diagnosed, when he went back to the little house on Pocahontas Avenue to get Lottie's portable black-and-white television set. He set it up on a table in her hospital room. He wanted to be angry with her for keeping it from him, but she seemed so frail now that his anger made him feel cruel. She made an effort to watch the ball games, but sometimes the doctors intervened and insisted that she sleep. So Billy watched them while she slept, and when she woke up, he told her all about how well Ewing and Wingate played. The night before the championship game one of the doctors asked him to step into the hallway. A beat-up folding chair sat against the wall outside Lottie's room in the oncology department of Rappahannock General. "You want to sit, Billy?" the doctor asked.

"Sure," he said, spreading the metal chair apart and sitting down. The doctor had Lottie's chart in his hand, but he did not open it.

"She's a tough woman, Billy, but she's about run her race."

Billy pushed his glasses higher up on the bridge of his nose. "What's she got, Doc?" he asked.

"It's called small cell carcinoma of the lung, Billy. Stage four."

"How many stages are there?" Billy asked.

"Only four. I'm afraid it won't be long now."

"How could I not know?"

"It can come on quick. Spreads like wildfire. Does she smoke?"

"Yeah," he said.

"Well, maybe you thought it was just smoker's cough. The honest answer is everyone reacts differently to it. She's had it at least a month or two given how extensive it is."

Billy stared at the opposite wall. "What happens after?"

The doctor grabbed a matching chair from down the hall and sat down next to him.

"There's a good place over Kilmarnock. They'll take care of her. However she wants."

"She's never said anything about it."

"The usual thing is okay, Billy, if she doesn't want to think about it now. It's a good way for folks to say goodbye."

"It's just me needs to say it."

"Well, that's okay, too."

Billy left his hat at home when he first drove Lottie up to the hospital and hadn't thought to grab it when he went to get the television. He wore a maroon T-shirt. The case for his glasses was stuffed into a pocket on his chest. He ran his fingers over the closely cropped hair on the sides of his head. He was the kind of man most people don't notice. The kind of man who tucks his T-shirts into his jeans. "Can I ask you something, Doc?"

"Course, Billy, fire away."

"You ever in the service?"

The doctor put his hand on Billy's knee. "She's had time to let the idea settle in. It won't be like that for her."

"But you know what I mean? You know why I'm asking?"

"The navy paid for me to go to Howard after I got back. They paid for MCV, too. I'm still trying to think of other stuff so they can get paid up on what I gave them."

They both smiled. "How'd you end up out here?" asked Billy.

"I grew up in the Northern Neck. Out Reedville way. Missed the water, I guess."

Billy laughed. "You still missed the water after being in the navy? I thought y'all would get enough of it out on those boats."

"No," the doctor said. "I was a corpsman. First Battalion, Ninth Marines. I'll tell you what, though, in July of '67" — he paused to whistle theatrically — "I damn sure wished I was on a ship."

"You know," said Billy, "when I was in Cambodia in '70, we'd be going through these rubber plantations and just getting shot all to shit, and I'd think sometimes, Maybe if I catch one it'll be just like I'm done being born. It won't be nothing worse than that. Just done being born."

"Yeah. Could be like that."

"You don't wonder? About after, I mean?"

"Sure, I do. I mean, I must. Every time I punch that clock I have this feeling. Not even a feeling. Something else. There's this voice that tells me one day I'm gonna punch that clock, and I'm gonna save all those nineteen-year-old jarheads I couldn't save at Con Thien when I was just nineteen myself. And I wonder, if I'm a man of faith, which I try to be, I don't do so well at it but I try to be, but if I am, then how come I worry after those boys still? They don't have pain anymore. Or hunger. But I can't help it. I always think they'd be better off here. Am I a bad man for wanting to drag them back? Is it a kind of selfishness? I guess I must be a little afraid of it, too. A place like this can fool you into thinking that you aren't afraid of it, but it's still there. I guess I can't say for sure how I feel about it. It's enough to make a man doubt."

They sat quietly for a while after that, but the conversation continued between them in the silence of their memories.

"She seems like a good woman, Billy," the doctor said.

"Better than I deserve, I'd say."

"Most people don't get half of what they deserve, good or bad. There's a lot I don't know about the world. And it's a hard thing going out into a world when all you know about it is how much you don't."

Billy leaned over the chair and cried. He was glad they were out in the hallway. He did not think Lottie would want to see him grieve this way, not because he ought to be ashamed of it, but because Lottie wanted Billy to be happy. He didn't want to disappoint her with his grief.

The doctor put his arm around his shoulders. He didn't say anything, he simply held him, not tightly, but firmly enough so that Billy did not doubt that he was with him in the present moment, as if it might be the thing that made a difference. "Listen up now, Billy," the doctor said, "when the time comes we're going to let her go, okay? That's what she wants. So you have to start letting go of her, too. It's gonna be hard. I know it is. But I want you to promise me something."

Billy broke down out there in the hallway, in a way he never had before, in a way he did not think could be brought back together. "What's that?" Billy said through his brokenness.

"Don't forget that you'll be living still."

The following night Billy sat next to Lottie's bed and turned the television on. The players on both sides hit their layup lines. The bands took turns playing. Lottie hummed the fight song. She knew the words by heart, but Billy could not make them out when the student section sang it. She rubbed one side of her face. "My eye keeps drooping here, Billy, look." It did; the pupil looked disordered, too.

"Let me turn the light down. The TV's bright enough for you to watch the game."

He had not seen the doctor that day. Billy thought he must have missed him when he drifted off in the chair beside Lottie's bed. There was something else he wanted to ask him, but he couldn't remember what it was. Nurses had come to check on Lottie, but just to make her comfortable, for pillow fluffing and the like. At tip-off, he saw she was asleep. She woke up once, ten minutes in, and said her ribs hurt. "Billy, I'd give it back to Adam if I thought it'd ease the pain a little."

"Gonna be a close-run thing, this one, dear."

She was not paying attention to the game. She was quiet, in and out of sleep. He didn't know if he was ready, but Lottie said she was. He decided to act the way a ready man would. Sometimes she chortled and twitched and sometimes she murmured.

Late in the second half it occurred to him he had not heard her for a while. Her breathing became ragged and she breathed now only at more distant intervals. It sounded to Billy like she was drowning in air. He looked over at her. They had been holding hands for the better part of two weeks, but late that night the strength went out of Lottie's grip. It had been a good strong grip. Lottie made things with those hands. Lottie made the world, Billy thought, and her leaving would unmake it. He prepared himself to fall apart again. To be unmade right along with the world. But he decided instead to live the way a good man would.

The volume was low. Villanova up by five with a minute

and a half left. He turned the TV off. The machines around her bed began to buzz and blink. A pinging bell. He put his hand on her cheek. Her mouth was open and her head tilted back a little. Billy squeezed her hand one last time and kissed her forehead and walked out the door. He rode the elevator down and went into the parking lot. He wanted to scream. Wanted to raise a noise that would put a dent in the heavens. But he didn't. He got into his truck and started the motor, letting it idle a bit before throwing the shifter into drive. He turned down Route 3 and headed back to Deltaville, to the house on Pocahontas Avenue. He parked and got out and walked to the edge of the riprap and looked over the bay. He looked into the void for hours, until the horizon was a long thin flame between the water and sky. When the sun came up, he turned his back on it and went into the house.

The nurses called the doctor in at 5:48 a.m. One of them opened Lottie's eyes and the doctor shined his flashlight into each pupil looking for a response. "I think that's it," he said. "Check her pulse, will you?" The nurse felt Lottie's wrist and shook her head. He scribbled in his chart. Lottie had long since left her silence in the room.

THIRTEEN

IN CHESTERFIELD COUNTY the summer of 1865 came and went. Autumn, too, took its harvest from the fields and departed. And winter returned without having to ask the way, and it spread out its blanket of snow over the endless now, as it had done always.

Emily watched the days pass through eyes tinged with gray and little flecks of gold.

Outwardly, she had become all sweetness and light. She no longer shuffled through the darkened hallways at night. When she went to sleep, she kept the curtains open, and in the mornings she rose when the first eastern light fell through the loblollies and onto her face. Her daughters blossomed, too. They had great big blue eyes and soft downy skin so pale that one might expect the winter light to pass right through it even after having traveled so far. She doted on them, and on little George as well, whom they all expected to speak soon. She made a great effort to leave Nurse with the impression that she now had a new, dutiful friend, saying, "Oh, I do wonder what he'll call me, Nurse.

There is such joy to be found when a child first starts saying names. They get them so wrong, don't they, but you can't shake them even so." But her face fell immediately after, and she allowed Nurse to see the sadness once again. "Would it be too much to ask you for a favor? I know you owe me nothing."

And Nurse replied as was required of her still, "Just ask and I will try, Miss Emily. I will try." George was laughing and the babies cooed in the dining room where the children sometimes played.

"Will you keep the girls with you if I ask?" She wiped small, perfectly formed tears from her cold flushed cheeks.

"Where will I keep them?"

"Wherever you are, have them with you, if I ask," said Emily.

"Can you tell me why?" Nurse asked. "The girls will want their mother. Look at them now. Their eyes follow you round the room."

"You know why, Nurse. You know. He is dormant now, but he will not be that way forever."

"I don't know what's come over her," said Nurse to Rawls one day that last December, "but I'll take it."

Rawls interrupted her. "I've known that girl a long time. And I've seen what kind of games she likes to play. You better keep your eyes open."

"You don't need to tell me that. But there's some things about being a woman, about being a mother in this world, that you can't understand. And to be married to that man, too? I think she's afraid of him, Rawls. And she has a right to be."

They were on a walk through the stand of pines where they'd first met. It no longer abutted the old plantation from which she'd been sent across the ice during that terrible winter when the James froze solid. Beauvais had swallowed it up. It seemed to Rawls that one day the boundaries of Beauvais would swallow the whole world. Levallois seemed to have a mind for it. After a while, Rawls thought, there wouldn't be a soul on earth who could recall a world different from the one Levallois was making for them.

"First you say it's the doldrums after a woman has a child. Now you say she's born again and all the funny stuff is just her being scared of Levallois. Well, that may be true, but I say sometimes a snake's afraid of other snakes."

Of course Nurse had seen all kinds over the years. Some lucky women place a child on their chest and it takes the latch right away, and life becomes a beautiful dream that both the child and the mother share. For others, the child is a great gift wrapped up in sadness; all they can see is the world the child has joined, how impenetrable its mysteries are and how permanent its pain. But these mothers seem to unwrap the sadness after a time, usually not longer than a month, or maybe two. And these mothers will see that the child is not afraid of the mystery, they have not yet learned that the pain is permanent, and the child will smile at the mother and she will look out on the world with a new faith, as if the child has told her that joy is not as infrequent a visitor as she thinks. And these mothers, like the first, will see the sun again, and in some deep fissure in their soul the idea takes root that their child may be the one who will unlock the world's terrible mysteries, or bring an end to pain, or bring joy with them as a frequent guest, and that though the conditions of the world may be very much as permanent and endless as the land on which we work, even those conditions can be improved with every season if worked rightly.

There are others, though. And for a flash after George's birth Nurse feared she might become one, as she had dreamed outside of time and seen the world drowned, the mountains thrown into the air and ground to dust. The idea came and left like lightning. How easily she could free him from how hard a day it would be today, how hard tomorrow would be, too. But George took to the latch right off. It was strange to her how easily she slipped into that first group. She had feared she would hate the child. No one would have judged her if she did not love him, but she did. And she would have not blamed Rawls if he did not love the child, but he did, too.

As for Emily, Nurse had watched her carefully, and as the children grew and smiled and crawled, and their mother got better and better at hiding the depths of her estrangement from the world, Nurse by instinct kept the children at her side. She had never seen it done herself, but she knew what the melancholy would sometimes tell a girl to do. "She's crossed that bridge, Rawls," she said. "I don't doubt that. But the road goes on. I just wish I had a better notion of where it's headed."

On the first day of the New Year of 1866, Bob Reid supervised as John Talbot moved the entire contents of the overseer's house out in the road: Bob's bed, a small oval table, a workbench, two upholstered chairs, every rag, and every last stick of furniture. It wasn't much, but it was all that remained for him to claim as his since returning from the war almost three years before. A dusting of snow covered the fields, and more fell on them as they worked. By noon they had everything loaded into two carts. They hitched a team of mules to each cart and Bob got into the first and John got into the second and they headed out toward the river road.

Nurse and Rawls came out from under the eave of the kitchen house to watch them, and Bob put the reins under his good foot and raised his hat to them with his left hand. They saw him talking to himself, though they could not hear him, and he was wildly animated in the driver's seat of the cart until he passed from view.

John Talbot came up behind him on the second cart. Rawls stepped out into the road. "What's all this now, John?"

"Can't say for certain. Mr. Reid says it's moving day. He says we're going to live at the old house. He spent the whole night talking bad on Mr. Levallois. Real bad. It was still dark when he woke me and said to put everything out for loading."

"What old house?" asked Rawls.

"Where y'all used to live at, he said."

"That house ain't even there no more. Nothing there but the train station now. Come on, John. Tell the truth, now."

John looked at Rawls and then at Nurse. His mouth hung open, a sign they both recognized as deep concentration. "Well, that's where he said we're going, so I guess we'll have a surprise when we get there."

"What'd he say about Mr. Levallois?"

"It's a lot of words I ain't supposed to say."

"What about the others?"

"Well," said John. "He said he's gonna kill him."

Nurse and Rawls looked at each other. Rawls stepped toward the cart holding his hand out, as if to help him down, but John did not seem to notice. "No," Rawls said. "You don't need to be involved in this foolishness."

Nurse stepped into the road and gently pulled Rawls back under the eave. Rawls looked at her and she shook her head at him. He went and sat down on a bench. "We've got work yet here, John, but you ought not go," Nurse said. "There's a world of ugliness gonna meet you there."

John pondered for a bit. "I told him I would." He finally said, "Besides, I've got half his things in the back of the cart. They're just gonna keep getting snowed on sitting here."

The three of them watched the first cart pass out through the last pair of cedars and turn toward the station. John slapped the reins at the mules, and the cart rumbled off to close the gap.

"What should we do?" Rawls asked.

"You know that place I told you about?" she said.

"You really want to go to look for a bunch of runaways on some islands in a swamp?"

"We're going," said Nurse.

234

"We don't even know what's out there. Could be just a story."

"It's real, Rawls. I know it is. And we're going. I don't know what's coming, but I don't want to be here when it comes."

They walked quickly toward their cabin. As they passed the house, Nurse looked up toward its hundred windows. From one of them, Emily watched as they went.

Bob and John Talbot pulled along the circle drive and halted their mules beneath the big sycamore tree. They began by carrying the upholstered items first, setting them up under the long roof of the waiting area behind the platform to get them out of the snow.

The station agent came out and asked them what was going on.

"It's just Mr. Levallois. He put it all in motion," said Bob.

The agent tucked away his curiosity on hearing the Frenchman's name and went inside. Trains came and went, but only a few, and the passengers' disinterest in the affairs of the two men placing furniture in the station merely confirmed a well-established fact: that people will ignore almost any aberration as long as it does not inconvenience them directly.

Bob did more directing than work, and his injuries were unforgiving nevertheless, and this made his hostility more general. By late afternoon they had a fair re-creation of the sitting room of the overseer's house at Beauvais Plantation. They had to let the diorama spill into the station agent's office a bit, at which fact John felt a great deal of consternation, but Bob slapped him on the shoulder when it was done and smiled and said, "We're well on our way, boy." He asked John to go back to the overseer's house to wait for him, saying they all might be together again soon.

John left the station. It was long after nightfall. His body ached from work and he was tired. He thought he'd like to go back to the overseer's house and go to sleep, and he began to nod off here and there even before the mules had left the pebble drive. He heard gunshots in the distance a little while later. Too many to count. He arrived in front of the overseer's house and went inside. He lit a fire and laid out his coat before it and went to sleep.

By the time the last train that left Levallois Crossing that night finally sparked its brakes and slowed to its destination the next morning, the news had made its way to Beauvais. Talk is as reliable as a coming sunrise, and in this case was a little quicker. Bob had shot eighteen people. The station agent, two disposable-bottle-cap salesmen en route to Fredericksburg, and a young couple with an infant were all killed. They said he reloaded several times, and that sometimes he seemed to aim and sometimes not, but all the same a dozen more people were wounded. Reports and gossip both agreed that afterward, as the crowd of travelers shook on the floor, and the smoke cleared out and a heavy silence took its place, he went about his business, setting a fire on the floor where his remade home lacked a fireplace, then carefully unfolded that morning's issue of the *Daily Richmond Examiner* and lit a pipe.

Slowly the uninjured got up from the floor. They ran off in little heats of two or three. When one of the last, lying just on the other side of the growing fire, got to his knees, Bob folded the paper down and said, "Excuse me, sir, are you leaving?"

The man quivered. He pissed himself. It spread in a little puddle from his left knee onto the floor. "Might I?" he asked.

"Of course. I'll see you later. But do tell everyone that Levallois's cruelty killed my wife. He stole my land from me. And my daughter, too."

"Yes. I will."

Bob folded the paper up and began to read again. "Good night, then," he said.

"Good night," the man answered politely, and got up from his knees and ran into the darkness.

Nurse and Rawls agreed to leave before first light. They had gone about their business so as not to attract attention to themselves and had gathered their things for the journey after dark. She washed her face that night in the basin's cold water and wrapped her hair in the same deep-blue-and-orange-blossom-flecked wrap she had worn when she'd first seen Rawls before the war, when her life was ordered by a more predictable cruelty. She looked down at him. He slept heavily, and her love for him stretched out on the bed alongside him. It was not so long ago. They were young yet. And though time has a weight that settles on one's shoulders with no regard for the ticking of a clock, she felt a new hope that they would finally find a life beyond Beauvais. Rawls did not love it there, of course. And though Beauvais was only a name, its good earth wore that name like a shackle. He had no servile affection for Levallois. And Bob and John Talbot and the girl Emily disappeared from his mind as soon as they were no longer in his presence. But if one were to tear down the walls of the plantation, and uproot all the posts in all the long miles of snake fence, and crumble the very foundations of every man-made thing to dust, there might be a place worth loving here, he'd said. But she could never accept that the place would not still be stained with blood, as even a wild place is when man has walked through it, though a man might think his walking is merely a passing through. I don't know nothing else but here, he'd said, when she'd brought up the idea of leaving before. I'm ashamed to say it, but I think I'd miss it some, he added. She replied that there was a whole world beyond the boundaries of Beauvais, beyond Virginia, beyond America, and she wanted to get a little of it before it was too late. And Rawls replied that her wants were his, that he would go anywhere with her as soon as she began to walk toward whatever that thing was, if only she would tell him what it was they were supposed to get a little of. Nurse smiled at the thought. They were on their way. The day had come. The people of Great Dismal would make a place for them as they had done for generations, and Nurse and Rawls would begin a new history for themselves along the dividing line between North Carolina and Virginia.

George slept curled at the foot of the bed. His arms were wrapped around Rawls's ankles and he used Rawls's crossed legs like a pillow. She opened the door as quietly as she could so they would not wake.

She saw Emily enter the wood line, making her way toward their cabin.

"I need your help, Nurse."

Nurse felt a desperate urge to resist her. To say that they were leaving and she must now fend for herself. But she knew that her resistance would call too much attention to her and Rawls to get away. "What do you need?" she asked.

"It's the girls," she said. "Something terrible has happened and I'm afraid Mr. Levallois will do something to me, or to them. Will you look after them here? You mustn't let him stop you."

Nurse ran through her options in her mind and saw how limited they were. "I'll get them," she said. She decided she would bring the girls to the cabin and place them in their little wicker bassinet. And she would put blankets over the bassinet so they'd be as safe and warm as possible until Emily came to fetch them. She hoped the children would not be left alone for long, but she would not miss her chance to leave this place forever. She and Rawls and George. They owed nothing to this place. Let this last gesture remove all doubt.

All his life, Levallois had been like a dog attuned to distant weather; his hackles up, his mood consumed with restlessness, always far enough ahead of the masses that they never thought to question how his desires became their reality. But Bob Reid had unleashed a terrible storm, and Levallois found himself caught out in it.

Bob didn't need to kill Levallois to ruin him, though it was clear he intended to draw him to the station to do just that. He only needed to diminish him. And if people began to question his authority, to wonder why they accepted his vision of the world as the only one possible, what would he have left? Mr. Levallois was a man, but he was also an idea. And he was an idea that no one in Chesterfield County had ever considered making an argument against. That is what he was truly afraid of; what would happen to him, to all his work, if they did? He shuffled through his desk and found a pistol. It was a gleaming, silver thing and he tucked it into his waistcoat. He sat at his desk, trying to figure his next move. He got up and slammed the door in frustration.

Emily listened from the stairwell and heard the lock tumble shut. She knew her father was not coming. He had no plan beyond revenge, but she had taken the threads he'd laid out on all those days they'd sat together on the porch of the overseer's house. She had worked and reworked them until they were woven into the fine cloth that would be finished that night. She had not known that her father would do what he had done, but she knew that he had given her an opportunity to put her plan in motion.

She walked briskly toward the overseer's house to find John Talbot. She looked through the front window and saw that he was sitting in the middle of the empty room, staring at the cold ashes in the fireplace.

She opened the door and went to him and kissed him. "Do you remember what I said to you by the river last summer, John, when you said you loved me?"

"You didn't say it back."

"I said that love is not a word, it's a demonstration."

He seemed to drift away, toward one thought or another. His mind was a small dark room, but it was a clean one, and Emily lost her patience with him before he found what he was looking for.

"It means you have to do something for me."

John Talbot thought of the river. And in his thoughts there was blood on a knife and Emily caressed him, and high bluestem grasses waved in a low spring breeze that shook the green buds on their branches. He wanted to choose a part of that past and leave the rest behind. He felt a tinge of uncertainty and he wondered if maybe the past did not allow that kind of choosing. "Do you think Mr. Reid is okay?"

"I would know it if something happened to him. He's my father, isn't he?"

"We'll go lay by the river again when it warms up?"

"It's all I want," she said.

"Tell me what to do."

"It's very simple, John. We're going to build a fire."

John Talbot watched from the porch of the overseer's house as Emily left Beauvais. She rode the big gray horse down between the cedars. She said she would be back to see the fire. Through the moonlit night, he saw Nurse walking toward the house. He saw Levallois standing in front of her, blocking her path. She tried to move around him, but he countered each move so that Nurse could not pass. Levallois pulled off her headscarf, the one John often told Nurse she looked so pretty in, and struck her. When she was on the ground he kicked her in the stomach. John watched it through the window from far away and no sound reached him. Emily had not said anything about this. Before sunrise, build the fire, she'd said. He repeated it to her, and then to himself all throughout the day. *Before sunrise, build the fire.* He watched Levallois pick up Nurse by the back of her dress and pull her to her feet. He could see her crying in pain, but he could not hear any sound. He carried Nurse deeper into the boxwood maze that led to the bare tobacco fields covered over with snow. He lost sight of them and then saw them again at the edge of the tree line that blocked the row of cabins from view.

She ought to be back, thought Rawls. How long did it take to scoop up those little ones and bring them here? He paced in the dooryard, kicking up little tufts of the carpet of pine needles and stomping down the miniature snowbanks that had reached the floor of the woods they lived in. He heard her coming first, wailing. He did not think he'd ever heard her make such a noise before. He heard her wail again. A crashing through branches. And then Rawls saw him. Levallois had her by the hair. She was tugging at his clothes. She had clawed his face and the blood ran down his cheeks. Levallois smiled. Rawls thought a devil would be no worse than him.

"Let her go," Rawls said.

He did. She collapsed into the wet needles behind him, weeping. Her right eye was shut. Her dress was torn. She saw Levallois's elk-handled knife in the needles just out of reach. He had not noticed it fall from its sheath as she struggled with him.

"Get away from here, Rawls."

"I'm not leaving her with you."

Levallois took the unblemished pistol out from his waistcoat. He cocked the hammer and pointed the barrel at Rawls. "Go, I said. Get the hell off my property."

Nurse crawled toward the knife and then stood up behind Levallois. She wrapped the elk-antler handle with both hands and brought it down toward his shoulder. He turned around to face her and dropped the pistol, reaching up to the wound from which his blood had already begun to fall into the snow. She stabbed him again. And then again. Time has a weight. Carrying it had made Nurse strong. Her lip was swollen and she did not speak or back away when he lurched toward her. Instead she stabbed him. He dropped to one knee. His cheeks were red, like the devil's, but he was only a man. Levallois did not talk. He breathed instead, hard and slow and steady as if he wanted to make sure he did not forget how to do it. Nurse stabbed him again and again until it seemed like little more than a nuisance to him. He tried to raise himself up, waving one arm behind him toward Nurse and the knife as if shooing a fly.

Rawls went to her and wrapped her in his arms. "He can't do nothing else to us," he said, "but we've got to go right now."

She stood there with the knife still clutched in both her hands. She was bloody to the elbows of her dress, but the blood was his. Levallois managed to bring himself to his feet. His right arm hung limp at his side, and his left searched his body for wounds, but there were too many to address one handed. "I'll go," he said, waving his good hand out in front of him. "I'll go. Just let me be." His knees shook and he swayed and his blood left a dark red circle in front of the cabin as it left his body.

Rawls, too, was unsteady on his feet, but he had let the ground show him its firmness over the years. Most people hardly noticed his strange shuffling gait anymore. Now he felt the pine needles underfoot, fallen so close to where all of it had happened. He felt the soil, too, and underneath the soil the dark red clay, and farther down the rock that had been the floor of a great sea. It steadied him. It lifted him up. He spun his hips and he felt rooted to the earth. He pulled his tobacco knife from the waist of his pants and swung with such force it made a wind that shook the snow from the pines. He buried the blade in Levallois's skull. It stayed there as the man fell dead.

John watched the moon recede in the sky above Beauvais. He walked to the shed behind the overseer's house and got a pick and two hoes and threw them over his shoulder. He walked down the hill and over the wide lawn and up the stone steps to the house's ornately carved oak doors. He put the pick through the door handles and barred the front. He went to the side of the house and did the same with the first hoe and then to the back with the second.

A quarter mile of ground lay between the big house and the overseer's place, but he crossed it quickly. The snow on the ground reflected the heavens, and the world seemed unusually bright to John, though the sun would not be up for a while yet. He listened to his footsteps and watched his breath form out in front of him in the cold night. He got back to the shed and found that he could tote three casks of coal oil in one go if he made his arms into a hoop and let the top cask sit tightly up against his chin. The first three he put at the farthest corner of the house and after three more trips it was well past midnight and his arms were tired.

She said to light the fire before sunrise when people were still asleep but not to worry because it would just be a big fire and no one but Levallois would be in there. He went to each corner of the house, put the torch to where he'd left the casks, and waited for the coal oil to get going on the cladding. He did not know how long it took for the fire to burn the way that Emily wanted, but it was a big fire now.

The flames illuminated the better part of Beauvais in the remaining night. The laborers came out to the wood line to watch. Fire shot up from the gables and hung from the high windows like the tongue of a man dying of thirst. John stood away from the flames, and the little snowdrifts disappeared and melted back from the house and left a blank circle of snowless grass. He heard things sizzle and pop inside, the shattering of glass. Soon there was nothing left for the flames to break. Fire makes a terrifying noise, thought John. It reminded him of crying children.

He walked back to the overseer's house and sat on the porch to wait for Emily. She had ridden away and said she would return, but she had not. Nurse and Rawls passed by on a buckboard. He waved to them. They looked at him but said nothing. He watched the brindle pony pull them away from Beauvais.

Rawls snapped the reins at the pony. George crawled from underneath the blanket they'd tucked him in for sleep. Nurse grabbed him and placed him in her lap. She put her arms around him and kissed his head. He stared at the fire. She took his head in her hands and turned it away from the flames. "Look away, George," she said. "Look away." And so they departed from Beauvais just as the sun broke the horizon to the east, in the first month of that New Year, on the second day of that first month; and in the darkness of that day they went out from Beauvais in the sight of all who watched it burn.

Three days later they reached a crossroad outside the town of Suffolk, Virginia. They could feel the nearness of their destination. Calm brown water stretched out beyond the flat fields. There was no snow here. The winter sun hung high in the cold blue sky. Tall white cypress trees stood with their roots beneath the water and there were islands dotting the distances beyond them. They turned the buckboard down the southeast spur of the road and drove it about a mile before a group of men emerged from the tree line and blocked their path, but one was not a man.

He looked to be a boy. His skin was pocked and his hair was the color of wet sand. His skin was also gray as were the coats the men wore and as were the boy's eyes like two dirty shards of ice behind his glasses. One of the lenses was cracked in a pattern that transfixed Nurse. He held a big curved knife in his left hand. The urge to look away from him was so strong she struggled terribly to hold his gaze, but she did hold it. They looked to Nurse like living ghosts, as if they had forgotten to stay down in their graves.

"Why you giving me that look?" he said.

"We just want to be on our way," said Rawls.

"Well, come on, then," the boy said. He spat on the ground.

"We ain't bothering nobody. We got no business with you."

"I don't much care one way or the other," the boy said.

Rawls pulled Levallois's gleaming pistol from his coat and pointed it at the boy. He pulled the hammer rearward and the cylinder shifted to the left, settling into place with an unmistakable sound.

The boy stared back at him. He worked a big rub of tobacco around his mouth and spit on the ground again. He did not seem to see the pistol at all. His companions spread around him in a ragged line, blocking the narrow road.

"You know what that is?" asked the boy.

Rawls didn't answer. He held the pistol as steadily as he could and kept it leveled between the two dirty lenses of the wire-rimmed glasses the boy wore.

"That's a showpiece. Can't hurt no one with that. Bigwigs give them out to folks so they can feel like they might do something with it. But it's just for show. Folks want to feel like they got a say in this world, so other folks give them the feeling, but they don't give them the say. Can't do nothing with a gun that shines like that but sell it or use it as a doorstop."

Rawls knew the boy was telling the truth, but he did not want it to end like that, so he pulled the trigger. The hammer fell with a click. Nurse flinched at the sound and so did a few of the men standing beside the boy. But the boy did not flinch. And Rawls did not flinch either.

"See?" the boy said.

They put up a fight. And Rawls was good and strong and so was Nurse. But they were few and the others many. In the end it did not take long. If only they could have faced them one by one, and name by name, but that is not what happened.

The boy took off his glasses. He whooped and yelped. He danced his dance.

FOURTEEN

IT WAS HARD to tell when dawn broke the day after the fire. Beauvais smoldered and its smoke filled up the winter sky, as if answering the fire that burned through Richmond the year before. Emily Reid Levallois stood in a distant tree line and watched as the same colonel who had come to Beauvais at the end of the war picked through the ruins of the house. Two Federals pulled her husband out of the pines near the workers' cabins and loaded him onto a cart. His shirt was stained the color of rust, and his limpness left little for her to doubt about his condition, but she did not know why he hadn't burned inside Beauvais.

She saw John Talbot on the porch of the overseer's house, shackled feet and hands. Though Emily did not know it, he was sitting in the same place that he had been found watching the fire when the soldiers arrived. She looked toward the kitchen house and then toward the stable but did not see any sign of Rawls or Nurse or the brindle pony Rawls rode or her daughters either.

She had expected her plan to set her free. But she had

never understood the meaning of the word until that morning, when the world revealed its inevitability and indifference to her, and she realized that her illusion of control was as impermanent as the ashes of the house now being sown over a thousand acres by the winter wind. An enlisted man with a shovel shouted to the colonel, and when the colonel arrived they sifted through the ash and removed a small, fire-blackened skull from the rubble. Emily sank to her knees. She wondered what would happen if she walked out of the tree line and feigned ignorance. Surely they were looking for her, if for no other reason than to see if she was among the victims of the fire. Emily did not know what happened to her husband; that was the truth. What story could she tell to undo what she had done? She watched the soldier pull another scorched skull from the fire. She tried to reconcile the small bones with the pale blue eyes the bones once held, eyes that had stared at her with an innocent and uncomplicated love, but she could not do it. She lay down in the wet leaves and buried her face in her arms, reckoning with the finality of what she had set in motion, and wondering if her father had unraveled like a use-frayed rope because he realized that some wrongs can never be set right.

A woman's face appeared before her through the trees. Emily recognized her but did not know her, except that she had been at Beauvais as long as she could recall. "Everybody's looking for you," the woman said.

Emily had nothing to return to and nowhere to go. "Don't tell them I'm here, please…," she said.

The woman heard her falter, searching for a name as she asked to stay hidden. "You don't know my name, Miss Emily, do you?"

"Please," said Emily.

The woman looked at her with a mixture of pity and disgust, then shook the branches and began to shout, "I found her! I found her! She's been hiding in these trees!"

Emily pulled herself up and ran toward the gray horse she'd left tied deeper in the woods. She turned the horse and mounted it and rode off, looking back only once to see the woman still shouting that she'd been found.

A week later John Talbot rode to the gallows in the back of his own cart. He sat on a plain pine coffin that he had fashioned himself from a loblolly felled out by the ferry landing. The colonel drove the cart, and a sergeant sat next to him. They allowed the dull boy to go unshackled to his hanging. They rode in the cart toward the courthouse, and a crowd gathered at the edges of the road along the way.

A New York paper sent a young reporter to cover the trial, as news of the bloodshed at Beauvais Plantation and the nearby train station had scandalized the Eastern Seaboard. He said the jury foreman later told him the jurors were "all farmers from around these parts, and when one of our animals goes crazy, we shoot it." But they were crazed themselves as they watched the cart take the killer John Talbot to his death. The colonel had looked for Nurse and Rawls but gave up quickly. John Talbot told him they had nothing to do with that night, that he alone had done what

Emily had asked him, and the colonel did not look for a reason to disbelieve him.

John Talbot was tortured with guilt when the nature and extent of his crimes were finally and clearly explained to him. He had done what had been asked of him, and she had not come back as she had said she would. He knew what that meant, and knew it down into the depth of his being, and this disordered his mind, shattering it like a poorly made cup. But still he slept at night. And though he seemed to some to have taken on a ghostly carriage in those last days before they strung him up, gray faced, his body moving with the slightest perpetual vibration, his gray eyes turned upward toward the sky in manner and color not unlike the smoke of a doused fire, that may only be because we will take any image and twist it into the thing we want to see.

John asked the colonel if he thought that Emily might come.

"I don't know, John," he said. In a way, he pitied the boy, and his thinking that if the girl came the world would have a chance at making sense again. But there was a kind of envy in him, too. The boy believed that it was possible. To make sense of it. To turn it over in your mind and discover that its mechanisms have an order to them. Maybe you could place the tip of your finger on the tooth of a gear and follow it as it turned. And you could see what else might move. And maybe if you looked very carefully at all the turning gears you could get back to the first one, to the first movement, the one that set all the rest in motion. But he had begun to doubt the world really worked that way. After sifting through the ashes of Beauvais, his certainty about the usefulness of order seemed grotesque, and he wondered if mankind might be immune to it by nature.

"The damnedest thing, Colonel," the sergeant said.

"What's that?" asked Tom.

"All this savagery out of nowhere."

"I don't think that's where it comes from."

They arrived and got John ready.

"You want the mask or no?" the sergeant asked.

"No, sir, I'll keep my eyes open."

"He's a light one, Sergeant," Tom said. "He'll need the long drop."

"They don't have the rig for it, Colonel. It's about three, four feet."

They tied weights to John Talbot's ankles. He could barely get up the steps without their help. The crowd was restless, their cheeks flushed with blood.

The sergeant moved toward the lever, but the colonel waved him off.

"I'll tell her you were asking after her if we find her, John."

"All right."

Tom pulled the lever. John Talbot fell out of the world.

~

The colonel did not find Emily, though he used all of the resources of his office for the balance of that year. No one found her. Normally we would say she was never seen again, but the fact is she was seen many times, though she was never known again by another living soul. Everything that would come to be said about her was true. And the truth has a funny way of making its way in the world. It was here before we crawled out of the sea. And it watched us from the tall grasses when we were naked and wandered the savanna and slept beneath the baobab trees. When there is one man or one woman left on earth, and they have sung their song and sit waiting for its answer, it will be listening. It does not need assent the way we do.

So yes, they saw her flitting among the Maroons of Great Dismal on their mesic islands, a white face among the black, as straight and slim a figure as the swamp's ageless cypresses. She was a washerwoman at a boardinghouse in Baltimore. She escaped the lynch mob and wound up passing through the two-bit cow towns along the western coast of Florida. And she spent her remaining days leaving tracks along the white sands where the Manatee River meets the blue-green stillness of the gulf. It is not so hard to imagine. The young Emily becomes older. Our certainty diminishes. Every day the same mismatched rows of least and royal terns look out toward a coming storm as small waves roll in and crash against the shore like the inevitable collapse of a trillion minor hills.

George, too, saw her once, but did not know it. By the early spring of 1906, he had left the Hugginses' home on the Outer Banks and traveled down to work the land near Tampa Bay. His would be among the first outfits to log the swamps around the bay for mangroves and buttonwoods. It paid good money and George hated to be cold.

He rented a room in Ybor City. In the warm air of late April, he walked to a park and unfolded his newspaper. The quake in San Francisco. It never ends, he thought. A woman sat on the bench next to his. She was older than he was, maybe fifty or sixty. But George could see that she was still a beautiful woman. Her skin was pale despite the sun, and her eyes were tinged with gray and gold. She spoke. Her voice was clear, but he did not hear the words. He leaned closer to listen.

The woman continued to talk. The sounds repeated. A litany. He leaned in again. "Are you okay?" he asked. "Do you need help?"

He did not recognize her, of course. How could he have? We are born forgetting, and our births and childhoods are soon enough dreams we can't recall. It's a kindness nature grants us, one of its few, because it lets us believe we are not made whole, that we'll have some say in the matter, when in fact our ending is written long before our beginning.

If she told him her name, there would be no spark of recognition, no trip into the past to hear it on the lips of his father. He would think to himself only that he'd always thought that Emily was a young girl's name. She seemed to not need anyone to listen, and she seemed quite comfortable performing her litany in whatever privacy the little park in Ybor City provided her. But George felt a curious premonition of regret, and so he folded his paper and went over to her.

She did not look up at him, did not in fact acknowledge him in any way. He thought he caught her midway through her procession. He listened to her for a long time. Over and over again the woman said, "You think you'll never love another thing in this world. And somehow it is there again. It comes from nothing and from nowhere. It comes from less than nothing. How does it happen? It is the only miracle."

ACKNOWLEDGMENTS

This book would not have been possible without the effort and dedication of the countless historians who make the preservation of our shared past their life's work. Though there is not enough space to express my gratitude to every person who has earned it, I would be remiss if I did not thank the following individuals and organizations explicitly. I am deeply indebted to my former neighbor Ace, whose generosity with his time and extensive knowledge of the history of Jackson Ward was invaluable to me, especially his stories of the period before and during the construction of the interstate highway system that so profoundly altered the neighborhood. I am also grateful to the staff of the Black History Museum and Cultural Center of Virginia, who have enriched my understanding of the city and commonwealth where I was born and raised. Many thanks are also due to M. D. Gorman of the National Park Service, whose expertise on Richmond during the Civil War is, in my humble opinion, unparalleled. His knowledge and passion for sharing it were particularly important in my visits to Chimborazo Park and the Chimborazo Medical Museum. To the employees and volunteers of the Library of Virginia, the Chesterfield Historical Society of Virginia, and the Robeson County History Museum, I would like to express my endless appreciation for your work. The resources the aforementioned people and institutions make available to the public are precious, and I suspect that without their efforts this knowledge would be lost. Whatever this book gets right about the times in which the events described take place, it does so in large part because I had their hard work to refer to. Whatever it gets wrong is my fault alone.

For their generosity, not just to me but to American culture at large, I want to express my gratitude to the John Simon Guggenheim Memorial Foundation. Without the support of their fellowship program, I simply would not have been able to do the work necessary to write this book.

I am also very pleased to have had the opportunity to continue working with Little, Brown and Company and want to express my gratitude to the following people there. To Michael Pietsch and Reagan Arthur, your continued support for my work means the world to me. To Lee Boudreaux, it has been a pleasure to have you as an editor, and a genuine relief to know I had your insight and experience to rely on. Betsy Uhrig and Sue Betz did a wonderful job copyediting the book; checking for factual inaccuracies, correcting numerous errors of grammar and punctuation, and keeping my inveterate inability to distinguish between "lay" and "lie" from being exposed to the world. Julianna Lee is responsible for the subtly beautiful cover design, which is quite possibly the very reason you picked up this book in the first place. If you heard about the book and became interested in reading it before seeing the remarkable cover, the excellent work of Little, Brown's marketing team, and of publicists Sabrina Callahan and Liz Garriga, probably had something to do with that. And to everyone else at Little, Brown who has had a hand in this book or either of my two previous books, I hope you know that I recognize what a real privilege it is to turn my writing in to your capable hands and watch you put it into the world.

To Peter Straus and everyone at Rogers, Coleridge and White, without your efforts on my behalf I would still be just a guy scribbling at a desk trying to figure out how the world works. That's still what I am, of course, but you have allowed me to do it as a profession. For that I am forever grateful.

My friends Shamala Gallagher and Philipp Meyer read early versions of this book, and their comments improved it immensely. I also want to thank my friend Roger Reeves for allowing me to use an excerpt from his extraordinary poetry collection *King Me* as an epigraph.

On a personal note, without my wife, Kelly, and two daughters, I would be lost. I won't try to improve upon that which Randy Travis has already perfectly expressed, so just know that I'm gonna love you forever, forever and ever, amen.

Most important, I want to thank anyone out there who has taken the time to read this book. I realize there are any number of things you could be doing with your time and money besides reading this, and I am genuinely humbled that you've chosen to spend it this way. My sincere hope is that you've found it worth your while.

ABOUT THE AUTHOR

KEVIN POWERS is the author of *The Yellow Birds,* which won the PEN/Hemingway Award and the Guardian First Book Award and was a National Book Award finalist, as well as *Letter Composed During a Lull in the Fighting,* a collection of poetry. He was born and raised in Richmond, Virginia, graduated from Virginia Commonwealth University, and holds an MFA from the University of Texas at Austin, where he was a Michener fellow in poetry. He served in the U.S. Army in 2004 and 2005 in Mosul and Tal Afar, Iraq.